Annie and the Outlaw

Montana Women, Book 2

By Nancy Pirri

Published by
Satin Romance
An Imprint of Melange Books, LLC
White Bear Lake, MN 55110
www.satinromance.com

ISBN: 978-1-68046-524-2

Cover Design by Caroline Andrus

Prologue

Christmas Day, 1887
Huntsville, Texas Prison

Cane Smith had a son.

A son.

The letter from Mae Franklin, dated a year ago, had found its way to him. During the six and a half years he'd spent in prison, he'd never received a single letter until now. There was a note tucked inside the envelope with Mae's from Judge Simon Hopkins, the man who'd sentenced him to prison. Mae had written the letter but had never sent it. In Bozeman, Montana, U.S. Marshal James Freeman, had found the letter addressed to Cane after Mae had been found dead in her home. She hadn't included an address but Freeman had recognized Cane's name from his trial and passed the note on to the judge.

Cane learned that a boy being raised in Bozeman by the Callahan family resembled Cane. The boy's mother, Giselle Hanks, had been a prostitute. She'd spent nights in the arms of many men, including Cane. On her deathbed, Giselle confessed to her friend Mae how she was certain Cane was her baby's father. Mae had asked her how she knew for certain, after being with so many men. Giselle's last murmured words convinced Mae. Only with Cane had she left herself unprotected, for she loved him and believed he loved her.

Tears welled in his eyes at the same time hope filled his heart. He had a son, a reason to live when he'd wanted to die. After spending almost

1

seven Christmases in prison, he had a purpose in finding a way out of this hellhole. He folded the letter and stuffed it into his shirt pocket. He lay back on his lumpy cot and imagined being a father—imagined what his life would be like with a son.

His happiness fled quickly at the thought of his life up to this point. How would he take care of the boy, even if he were released? He'd been a wandering cowboy for years before going to jail. He was twenty-eight years old and had accomplished nothing good in his life. Nothing except for fathering a child.

Cane thought back to the day he'd been sentenced to twenty years in prison—for a train robbery he hadn't committed. Without proof, he never had a hope in hell of clearing himself. The few folks on the train who'd witnessed the robbery had accused him.

Was there a chance of turning it around now? He had to find a way. Sitting up with renewed determination, he decided he'd find a way out of prison and claim the boy. He came to his feet. "Hey! Jailer!"

The only reply he received was from the inmate in the cell to his right. "You prick! You woke me up."

Old Warren Strom was no threat. Truth be told, he was Cane's only friend in this godforsaken place. "Sorry, Strom, I need to see a guard."

"What for?"

"I need to write a letter and don't have any paper or pencil."

A hand holding a scrap of paper, a yellowed envelope and a broken stub of a pencil appeared out of the bars at the front. Cane reached over and grabbed them. "Thanks. I owe you."

Strom muttered gruffly, "Now shut the hell up and let a man get some sleep."

Settling down on his bunk again, Cane wrote back to the judge. When he finished, his heart felt weighed down in grief as he thought about sweet Giselle who'd died, strangled by some drunken cowboy passing through Bozeman shortly after the birth of their son. The poor woman hadn't had any chance in life, having been born of a prostitute, the only home she'd known a brothel.

He'd been no better than any other man who'd swaggered through her boudoir door. After living on the plains for weeks at a time, spending a night with a prostitute was one of the few joys in life a cowboy had to look forward to when he came to town. A few visits to Giselle, and he knew he'd fallen in love.

The last time he'd seen her he promised he'd return once he saved enough money. Then he'd marry her and take her away with him. He thought of her tear-filled eyes and the longing in them as she'd nodded. It was only after he left town that he realized she hadn't believed him for an instant. He guessed she'd received similar offers from other cowboys who hadn't kept their promises. He'd meant to keep his and would have if he hadn't gone to jail. Sadness filled him then as he thought of Giselle dying before he could show her he meant his declaration of love.

Cane hadn't been able to save the woman he loved, but, by God, he would find a way out of prison and find his son.

He thought about Judge Hopkins, the man who'd deliberated over his trial. He'd come to know the judge a bit the few times he'd come to Bozeman before being accused of the train robbery. Had sat and drank a beer with him and played a few hands of cards. From that little interaction, he knew the judge was a good, honest man. Before Cane went to prison, after his trial, the judge had taken him aside and said he believed in his innocence. Unfortunately, the jury hadn't. Then the judge had told him to keep his ears and eyes open while in prison.

Prisoners came and went—none of them shedding any new information—until a month ago, when two new prisoners had arrived. Prisoners were allowed out of their cells only a few hours a day. Cane was watchful, planting himself near these men to hear more talk whenever he could. The longer he listened to them, and the more he watched them, he began to recognize them. They'd been two of several cowboys working a cattle run with him before he was arrested. One of the men bore a striking resemblance to Cane.

In the letter he'd just written, Cane asked Judge Hopkins to open his case once more, based on what he'd heard. Meanwhile, he would keep his ears open for more information. He'd befriend the two men, hoping they'd take him into their confidence.

Chapter One

October 1888
Bozeman, Montana

Annie Callahan sat patiently, waiting for her seven-year-old-brother, Mark, to leave the schoolhouse, even though she had chores to do at the ranch. Waiting for Mark was never a waste of time. Besides, these precious moments gave her the opportunity to mentally organize all of the tasks she needed to complete in preparation for the holidays.

She'd already started sewing chambray and woolen shirts for the ranch hands, a tradition that had been passed on to her from her mother, and a task she thoroughly enjoyed. She still had several more shirts to sew for the men, plus the new pants and shirts for her brother. She smiled. Unlike the ranch workers, Mark wasn't as excited about getting new shirts. His Christmas wish list included a gun, slingshot, a bow and arrow, and a tomahawk. The thought of Mark handling a weapon made her shudder.

Suddenly, like lightning on a stormy night, a premonition struck Annie from where she sat outside the schoolhouse in her wagon. She saw herself sitting on the ground. A man's shadowy form stood over her. She fought to remain conscious; fought to ascertain the man's identity.

No!

She didn't want to know him!

Pull yourself out of it, Annie!

Forcing away the presence, the man disappeared and sanity returned. Breathing easier, she blinked several times. Looking around at the calm, peaceful schoolyard, she breathed a sigh of relief. She was still sitting on the bench in her wagon, her horse's reins gripped tightly in her hands.

She tugged her shawl close around her shoulders to stave off the cold, wishing Miss O'Gara would release the class. The temperature had been tolerable during the day but, with the lowering of the sun, the air had grown chilly.

Suddenly, searing pain pierced her skull. She slammed her eyelids shut and collapsed against the back of her seat as the premonition returned, full force this time.

A man with a muscular build stood over her as she clutched Mark in her arms. Her eyes widened in horror when he bent closer. She saw nothing but his shadowy form, unable to make out his features. He reached for her brother, big hands stretched out, fingers clawed. Screams tore from her throat. Her mind screamed, Run! *But she couldn't. Her feet seemed to be locked in place. The man wrestled Mark away from her and fled, her brother's screams piercing the air. Sobbing inconsolably, she remained helpless as the child's shouts dimmed.*

Annie's breathing calmed as the premonition faded away. Nevertheless, she kept her eyes closed. No, Mark was safe. He was here, in school.

She had no desire to look into the future, no desire to feel any pride or satisfaction in the "gift" God had given her. Why He'd chosen her, she had no idea. Due to skepticism in town from some, fear and suspicion from others, she'd learned to keep the premonitions to herself. She guessed if hunting witches were in fashion, she'd be gone from this earth by now.

A door creaked, and Annie looked up to find the door wide open. Then the schoolchildren poured from the building. Still, Mark didn't appear, but she knew the teacher was helping with his arithmetic for a few minutes after school.

She looked around again and saw a man walking toward her. Seeing him pause as he watched the children scattering in all directions, she shivered.

With the sun low in the sky behind him, she saw only his silhouette. Apprehension settled in. Could it be the man she'd just seen in the vision? The man's hair was dark as the night, framed by a black Stetson. The

5

closer he came, the more she saw of him. She noted that the color of his hair was identical to Mark's.

"Miss Annie Callahan?"

"Yes." At his low, raspy tone, she froze in her seat. "Are you here for a student? I'm afraid they've all left for the day."

Removing his hat, he strode toward her, then stopped beside her wagon. "I'm here for my son."

"As I said, they've all gone home. I'm just waiting for my brother."

His son, he'd said. She knew everyone in Bozeman, but not this man. Her heart stalled at the handsome, square-jawed face. His dark eyes were hard and searching. His finely chiseled lips made her wonder for an unbidden moment what their touch would feel like. She also caught the weariness etched in his face, and the thick, dark hair that bristled along his jaw and on his chin. He appeared as though he'd been away from civilization for a while. A shave and haircut were certainly in order.

She swept him another look from head to toe. Never had she seen such a tall man save for her neighbor, Jed Porter. Lately Jed had gotten pushy about trying to court her, forcing her to be firmer in declining his suit.

The man drew even closer, and she stiffened once more in her seat.

She stood up despite the awkwardness in the wagon. "Who are you?" Because no evil thoughts entered her mind, no premonitions concerning him filled her heart and soul, just those few shivers, she guessed this man wasn't violent and would do her no harm. But then she hadn't seen the features—only the shadowy bulk—of the man in the premonition she'd had...

"My name is Cane Smith, and I've come for my son."

She frowned. "What's his name, sir?"

"Your family named him Mark."

~ * ~

Cane Smith grimaced when he saw her face drained of all color. "Miss Callahan? Maybe you should have a seat."

"Yes," she whispered.

She just stood there, showing no signs of heeding his advice. Reaching up, he gently took her elbow and pulled her back down on the

6

bench seat. Breathing in deep, he enjoyed the sweet honey scent of this pretty, fair-haired young woman.

Eight months of befriending the bastards he believed committed the crime he'd been accused of had finally afforded Cane the proof he needed. In front of several prisoners and a few guards, the braggarts confessed they had indeed robbed that train. The prisoners and guards had promised Cane they'd stick up for him when he went to court with the new evidence. In late August, Cane had his day in court and, after all testimony was given, was finally released. He made it a point to find Judge Hopkins once he arrived in Bozeman to thank him, and to claim his son.

Heaven help the man or woman who stood in his way—even this Callahan family who'd taken the boy in.

Upon his arrival in Bozeman, he'd inquired in town about the Callahan family. Katie Freeman, proprietor of Katie's Palace, informed him that the Callahan family lived several miles outside of town on a spread called the Moonstruck Ranch. She also informed him Annie worked at Katie's Palace and had just gone to pick up her brother at the schoolhouse on the outskirts of town. Cane left Bozeman on foot, since he had no carriage or horse, to meet Miss Annie Callahan and his son.

He settled his hat on his head, watching her gather her composure. When she rose, he assisted her down from the wagon. She stood before him, the sweetest confection of womanhood he'd ever seen, with tears in her eyes.

He couldn't see much of her since she had averted her gaze. After a moment, she visibly squared her shoulders, tossed back her head and glared up at him. "Mark may be your son by birth, but my father and I have raised him since infancy. He's a Callahan now."

Cane felt his face turn hot as he straightened to his full height. First irritation, then anger, flared through him but it quickly subsided. If he'd learned anything in prison, it had been the virtue of patience, which would serve him well for the rest of his life. Long gone were the angry, impetuous days of young manhood.

"He's a Smith, and he'll soon learn the fact of the matter. And there's nothing you can do to stop me from telling him."

She jammed her index finger into his chest. He stumbled back a step out of sheer surprise.

7

"No, you can't claim him! You aren't the one who fed him, clothed him and changed his diapers. You aren't the one who stayed up all night caring for him when he was ill and burning up with fever," she choked out.

She reacted much as a mama bear would when her cub was threatened. He liked that; liked how she had so much love for his son. It meant that she and her father had cared for him well. Cane ached for her…just for a moment.

It was time to make the woman understand he wasn't backing down, though he had to admit he admired her lack of fear of him.

He took a step forward, and she backed up a step but still kept her chin tilted up at him. *Stubborn woman!* He saw unshed tears sparkling in her eyes and groaned inside. Tears were the worst weapon she could use on a man, especially this one.

Cane tried reasoning with her. "By no choice of my own did I not claim him earlier. I want to experience everything I can now. It's my right. He's mine." Cane had been born illegitimate himself and never knew his father. He wouldn't allow that to happen to Mark.

"No!" she wailed. "My father adopted Mark. He won't let him go without a fight."

"I understand. If I were your father, I'd do the same. If you don't mind, Miss Callahan, I'd like to speak to him now, as soon as Mark comes out."

Cane wound his hands around her tiny waist and lifted her easily onto the seat of her wagon. Off balance, she plunked down hard on the seat and grimaced. She gasped but held her tongue. Sitting in the driver seat, her eyes focused straight ahead, tears tracking down her cheeks.

"He might fight me, but, when all is said and done, Mark will be mine. I came all the way from Texas to claim my son."

Cane understood men better than women. He'd spent most of his life with them and quite frankly knew little about the fairer sex—with the exception of prostitutes who'd serviced him when he needed a woman. He'd spent months crossing the country without fair company, except for the occasional town he passed through. And, when the opportunity arose to spend a night in a willing woman's arms, Cane, like most cowboys, took it.

8

He guessed, in the end, Tom Callahan would give Mark up. He would understand that the boy belonged with his true father.

"I need to get home," she whispered.

"I'm riding with you, so scoot on over."

She scanned the area, then looked at him. "How did you get here?"

"I walked."

"From the stagecoach depot?"

He nodded.

"Why, that's three miles!"

"A mere Sunday stroll," he said dryly. "I told you that I'm claiming my son. Nothing can keep me from him. Now move on over."

She obliged him.

Good. The woman was sensible and smart. He smiled to himself. She was far from the quiet type. The element of surprise had changed what he guessed was usually a confident, bossy woman. But he'd also heard the softness in her voice, especially when she spoke about Mark.

He wasn't fond of the name Mark, but hell, the boy was nearly eight now. Mark he'd remain.

The school door swung open, and a child's voice shouted, "Annie!"

He centered his attention on a boy running toward them.

Mark! Cane recognized himself in the boy who had to be his son tearing down the walkway with black hair flying and dark brown eyes filled with joy. Then he noticed how Mark's gaze was riveted on Annie. Turning toward the woman next to him, Cane's heart wrenched at the aching love he saw on her face. For a fleeting moment, he had doubts about taking the child away from her and the only life he'd known since birth.

He hardened his heart. He deserved some happiness, some love in life, damn it all. He would find it with his son.

He hungrily watched Mark while the boy ran to Annie's side of the wagon. She helped him scramble up onto the seat, then hugged him. Cane watched her take him into her arms, saw her breathe in deep to catch his little boy scent. Once again, Cane's heart ached to hold the boy, but he couldn't. He would have to take things slowly.

"You learning your arithmetic?" She tousled the mop of dark hair.

9

Mark nodded then pulled out of her arms and jammed his hands against the sides of his head. "No scrubbing my head! It's not bath time."

She laughed.

Cane was caught, mesmerized by how she looked even younger and prettier, as she grinned at his son.

The boy slanted his gaze away from Annie, turning serious when he faced Cane. His son stared at him for the longest time, his gaze riveted on him. After a while, he said, "You have black hair like me."

~ * ~

Annie's heart started racing at Mark's words, and she saw the curious look in his eyes. It'd only been in recent months that he'd questioned why his father and sister had blonde hair while his own was black. Until he grew older, Annie and her father had decided they'd wait to tell him about his parentage, though they had informed him in the past year that they'd adopted him. She'd easily managed to divert his attention in the past but guessed it wouldn't be easy for much longer. Especially if Cane Smith had his way.

"Yes, it is. Almost the same exact color." Cane held out his hand. "I'm Cane Smith, a friend of your sister's. I'll bet you're Mark, aren't you?"

"Yep." Mark pumped Cane's hand, squeezing it as tight as he could. "Mark Callahan."

Cane's smile widened while he shook the boy's hand. Annie couldn't help but notice that Mark was a "chip off the old block." Releasing Cane's hand, Mark looked at Annie again.

"Can we go home? I'm hungry!"

"Of course! Mr. Smith is driving us home tonight. He'll be having supper with us. How does that sound?"

"Great!" Mark shouted.

"Then let's be on our way," she said.

Mark settled between the two of them on the wooden seat and Cane snapped the reins to get the horse moving.

"What do you think Mrs. Williams made us for supper?" Mark asked.

"Mrs. Williams is under the weather today, so I'm cooking supper, honey."

Mark's eyes widened. "You are?" At her nod, he yelled, "Yippee! I like your cooking a lot better."

"Mark! Mrs. Williams is a wonderful cook."

"But not like you, Annie." The boy turned a brilliant smile on Cane. "Annie makes the best fried chicken, and taters and cornbread."

"Sounds mighty good," Cane said.

To Annie's mind, the man looked about ready to salivate. She wondered when he'd eaten last. She glanced at Mark. "How did you know I was making chicken?"

"Saw Pa kill a chicken this morning."

"You watched?"

"Yup, sure did. You shoulda seen Pa wring his neck, then chop its—"

"Enough. I believe you. Father knows I don't want you watching such violence."

"It's not violence," Cane interrupted.

Her eyes widened. "Excuse me?"

"Nope. It's a natural life cycle for an animal that we use for sustenance. Mark needs to learn these things. Your Pa's right to show him."

She frowned. "That may be, but not yet. Mark's only seven years old."

"Old enough." Cane looked at Mark. "While your sis is cooking, we can talk and get to know each other."

Giving Cane a coy look, Mark asked, "You play checkers?"

Cane nodded. "Sure do."

"Woo-hoo!" Mark whooped with delight.

Annie smiled at Mark's exuberance and glanced at Cane. He wore the biggest smile. The stone-faced, taciturn man's expression softened as he gazed at Mark. She found it hard to believe him capable of having a soft bone in his body—for anything or anyone.

The wagon rumbled through town. They were just passing Katie's Palace when Annie saw her friend Katie Freeman step outside with a broom, her two-year-old daughter, Melanie, on her heels with a smaller broom in hand.

Mark hollered, "Hi, Mrs. Freeman! Hi, Melanie!"

Katie waved and called out, "How you doing, Mark? Annie?"

"Stop a moment, please," Annie said.

Cane stopped the horse in front of Katie.

Katie leaned on her broom. "Any chance you can serve on Saturday, Annie?"

"Serve, not cook?"

"Doc says since I'll be having this baby any day, I need to put up my feet more often." She grinned. "Tough to do running this place though. After I have the baby, I know I'll need even more help. Judge Hoskins knows of a woman who needs employment so I'll be meeting with her soon. For now, it would help if you served and I cooked. Think you can help me out on Sundays, too?"

"I'll tell Father that you need me the extra hours. Are you and James prepared for the new baby?"

Just then, Katie's husband, James Freeman, ambled outside. Pausing beside Katie, he took the broom from her hands and set it against the building. He scolded her, "Didn't doc say you need bed rest, not work?"

Katie rolled her eyes. "Yes, but I'm going stir crazy!"

He hugged her as close as he could with her expanded stomach. "I know, but it won't be for much longer." He glanced up then. "Hey, Annie. How are you?"

"Just fine, thank you." Annie looked between the two of them; saw the mock scowl on James's face and the frown on Katie's brow. "You two are more than ready for that baby to be born, aren't you?"

"Baby!" Melanie exclaimed, excitement in her eyes.

James lifted Melanie in his arms, laughed and rubbed noses with her.

Annie laughed, marveling at the likeness between Katie and Melanie. Almost nine months to the day after James and Katie married, they had Melanie. It took another few years of praying for another child before Katie was pregnant again. Annie looked at James and saw his curiosity as he stared at Cane.

Where are my manners?

"Oh, uh, Katie, James? This is Cane Smith, newly arrived from Texas."

James stepped forward and reached across Annie. "We've met before, briefly," James said.

Cane took James's hand. "Thanks for passing on the letter to the judge. I appreciate it."

"No problem." James stepped back from the wagon and looked at Annie, then Cane. "How long you going to be in Bozeman?"

"I'm staying permanently. Looking for some land to raise cattle and horses."

"When you get a chance, take a look at the Ames place south of here twenty miles or so. It just went up for a sale. It's a prime piece of property, so I don't expect it to be unsold for long."

Cane nodded. "Thanks for the tip."

"We need to get home," Annie said. She smiled at Katie. "See you Saturday."

"I really do appreciate your help, Annie." Katie's gaze slid to Cane. "So how long have the two of you known each other?"

James warned, "Honey…"

Annie laughed. "I should have mentioned that we just met. Cane has business with Father."

"I see," Katie said.

Annie met Katie's curious eyes and tried communicating through her own. *I'll tell you later.* "We have to get home for supper."

"I'll see you Saturday then."

Cane tipped his hat to Katie and a nod to James before slapping the horse's rump with the leads. The sun had nearly set by the time they reached the Moonstruck Ranch. Mark scrambled down from the wagon and tore into the house. "Pa! Pa! We're home, and Annie's cooking us supper!"

Annie went to leave the wagon and found Cane standing with his arms raised to help her down. She bit her lower lip with indecision. He made the decision for her when he wound his hands around her waist and easily plucked her from her seat. "I don't bite," he said softly.

She raised her brow. "Oh! That's good to hear."

Cane chuckled. Annie's face heated up in embarrassment.

On the ride home, she'd thought about the premonition at the schoolhouse. Could this be the man threatening to take Mark from her?

13

Chapter Two

Cane liked the fact she was cautious around him. Caution had been his friend on more than one occasion. He took Annie's arm, ready to release her if she showed any signs of reluctance. When she didn't, he was surprised. He frowned then and thought most everyone who crossed his path, before and after his imprisonment, was wary around him.

She held up her skirt as she climbed the steps ahead of him. Cane gulped when he saw her slim, delicate ankles. Lordy, but she was a beauty, and such a lady. Reaching around her, he opened the door to the big ranch house, and she swept in ahead of him.

He stood uneasily in the hallway with his hat in his hand. The interior of the house held a gracious yet rustic quality, same as the exterior. Highly polished wood floors smelled of wax. To the right was a large, square dining room with a beautifully crafted table and chairs covered in fabric-tufted cushions. A chandelier dripping with small crystals shone with a warm sparkle. He saw several open doors to his left and guessed these led to other rooms such as a parlor, library and, of course, the kitchen.

"Wait here while I find my father," Annie said and rushed down the hallway.

Suddenly he felt self-conscious in his dusty dungarees and sweat-stained chambray shirt. He touched his bristly jaw-line and grimaced. He should have gotten a place in town where he could shave and clean up before he went hunting for his son. Too late now.

He saw the second door down the hall open. A short, muscular man with blonde hair and graying temples, dressed in shirtsleeves strode toward him. Annie followed. Cane braced himself, ready to battle the man until he caught a twinkle in the older man's eyes despite his serious expression. Cane liked Annie's father immediately.

"Annie doesn't often bring company home." The man offered his hand, and Cane shook it. "I'm Tom Callahan."

"Cane Smith. Annie probably told you we need to talk."

Callahan nodded.

While the man didn't make it obvious, Cane caught the older man's swift, assessing gaze and straightened up, silently waiting for the older man's condemnation.

"Come into my library."

Cane followed Callahan, Annie at his side. Outside the library door, he stopped short and took his daughter's hand. "Go see to supper, honey."

"But—"

"I'll let you know all that we talked about later."

Cane saw the gentle but firm look on Callahan's face. Cane expected fireworks to start any moment. Cane had seen his share of headstrong women in his life and he expected this spitfire to protest. Annie's face clouded with indecision, then she gave a curt nod. Surprised, he watched her turn on her heel to leave them.

"Mr. Smith?"

Cane felt heat rush into his cheeks when he found Callahan waiting, watching him. Cane lurched into a library, filled floor to ceiling with books on three walls of the room. Astonished, Cane could only stare at the volumes, his eyes and mind eager to delve into them one at a time.

Behind him, Callahan said, "Please, sit down. So, you claim to be Mark's natural father. What proof do you have?" Callahan took a seat behind a desk.

Cane set his hat down on a corner of the desk and sank into a seat across from Callahan, digging inside his shirt pocket. He pulled out the letter encased in its envelope and handed it over. He watched the older man peruse the address on the envelope before removing the letter. He unfolded it and read it. Within moments, he looked at Cane and heaved a deep sigh.

"It appears what you say is true." Chagrined, he added, "Truthfully, from the moment I laid eyes on you, I knew Mark was your blood kin. You know it'll be difficult to pull him away from Annie, don't you?"

Cane nodded. "She seems real attached to the boy."

"Correct observation. I am, too, of course. Why were you in prison, son?"

"Train robbery."

"I'm assuming you didn't do it since you're a free man now. Or are you?"

Cane didn't expect the question and hesitated in replying for a moment. "It was a case of mistaken identity. When I finally had the evidence to clear myself, I wrote to Judge Hopkins, who re-opened the case and freed me."

"After all these years," Callahan said. "Wish you'd gotten out sooner. We've had Mark with us since a few days after his birth. Needless to say, he's part of our family."

"I know. I'm sorry." Cane's eyes felt gritty. "I've no home and not much to offer Mark, but I am his father. And I promise I'll do everything I can to make a good home for him."

"But will you be able to love him?" Callahan softly inquired.

"I already do."

Callahan studied Cane. "I believe you. So how do you plan on making a home for him?"

"I like Bozeman. I'm thinking of settling here. I heard there was land for sale. Have you heard of any good acreage?"

"For sure there are several parcels. I'll get hold of a newspaper so you can check them out. I noticed you came here with Annie and gather you've no horse or wagon?"

"No. I'll buy a horse in town tomorrow."

"I've horses for sale you may want to take a look at."

"I'll do that. Now maybe you can give me some advice as to how to get Mark from your daughter's clutches."

Callahan laughed. "I'll talk to her, but you know she's got a real stubborn streak."

"Hmm, she didn't give you any grief about not sitting in on this meeting."

"Yes, I've got to admit her compliance surprised me."

"How so?"

"It means one of two things. She's getting' her eggs in order and making plans to fight us, or she's in agreement with us."

"I've a feeling it's the first one."

"You may be right." Callahan rose from his chair. "This may be easier than it seems. We recently informed Mark that we'd adopted him as an infant."

"That's good," Cane said.

"Don't discount the fact though that it'll still be difficult pulling Mark away from the only family and home he's ever known. I suggest we do this in stages."

Cane frowned. "Now how would we do that? We tell him or we don't, and the second is not an option."

Callahan nodded. "I understand, but it would behoove all of us to take this slow and easy. We don't want to frighten him. He'll be confused enough once we do tell him."

Cane stood as well. "Sounds reasonable, and, since I do plan on staying in the vicinity, I don't think that should be a problem."

"Good." Callahan walked with Cane to the door. "Once Mark gets used to seeing you around, once he grows comfortable around you, we'll tell him. It'll be hard for him, though, no matter what and when."

"Yes, I suspect it will, but he'll adjust."

"Eventually," Callahan replied.

"What exactly do you propose at that point?"

Callahan swung open the door. "Allow me to think about it overnight. We'll meet up again in the morning."

"Then I'd better head back to town. I haven't found a room yet."

"Nonsense! You're our guest. Stay as long as you like—even until you get your own spread. We've plenty of room here." A broad smile covered Callahan's face. "It's nearly time for supper, Mr. Smith." He took a deep breath, then released it. "Do you smell that chicken? And baking powder biscuits?"

"Call me Cane. And, yes, I do. Better than anything I've smelled in years."

Callahan led the way to the kitchen. "Yes, my Annie's one of the best cooks around. Not only does she take care of the house and cook, she works at Katie's Palace, in town, cooking meals."

"Yes, I met the owners, James and Katie Freeman today."

17

"Good," the older man nodded. "Yessir, Annie will make some man a wonderful wife someday."

"I'm sure she will, sir," Cane muttered, pulling at his collar uncomfortably as he followed Callahan down the hallway.

Eating supper like a civilized human being, sitting at a table, made Cane squirm inside. He'd spent years in a jail cell, eating scraps off a tin plate with his fingers. Prisoners weren't allowed eating utensils for fear of "picking" their way out of jail, or injuring or killing a guard.

Cane passed through the dining room and paused in the kitchen doorway. His gaze fell on Mark who squirmed in his chair, tapping his fork impatiently on the table. Cane smiled. He recalled being seven—nearly eight—and being so hungry he'd done the same thing...until his mother scolded him to sit still like a gentleman.

Then he looked at Annie who stood at the stove, forking pieces of cooked chicken from a cast iron skillet onto a platter. They were golden brown and steaming hot. Suddenly, Cane's stomach rumbled so loudly all eyes settled on him.

"Sorry," he muttered as he stood awkwardly in the doorway. "Been awhile since I last ate."

"Then take a chair," Callahan said. "Hope you don't mind the informality of eating in the kitchen. Unless we have company, there's no point hauling the food into the dining room."

"But, Pa, Mr. Smith *is* company!" Mark said.

"Uh, that's true," Callahan said. "If you prefer..."

Cane replied, "The kitchen's fine with me."

"Guess I'm inclined to include you as family, Cane," Callahan said.

"Me, too!" Mark grinned at Cane.

Cane glanced up and caught the frown on Annie's face as she moved to the table with a platter in hand. Apparently, *she* wasn't ready to think of him as family.

Cane pulled out a chair beside Mark and sank into it. Callahan sat at the head of the table.

Silence ensued when Annie placed the chicken in the center of the table. She reached for the chair opposite Cane and Mark. Cane scrambled from his seat and tore around the table, bumping into Annie in order to hold her chair for her. Grateful for the gentle smile she gave him, he didn't feel like quite the bumbling idiot when she sat down and he eased her close to the table.

In his own seat once more, he started to reach for his fork but quickly pulled his hand back upon seeing the others bow their heads.

"Heavenly Father, we thank You for the excellent food, provided by Your generosity, and for the guest at our table tonight. Amen," Callahan prayed.

They ate supper, and it was only after Cane had taken his fourth piece of chicken that he realized the silence. Looking up, chicken leg in mid-air, he met Annie's wide-eyed expression. He glanced at Mark, who was happily gnawing on a chicken leg, meeting Cane's eyes with a gleaming, satisfied look in them.

He lowered the chicken leg to his plate. Picking up the linen napkin on his lap, he swiped at his mouth and sat in silence, feeling self-conscious. He'd made a pig of himself, but he hadn't eaten much since going to prison, and he sure hadn't eaten any better since his release. He'd been on a mission to find his son and had eaten little in the last week. Now that he'd accomplished that deed, he'd given in to his hunger.

"Hey, Mr. Smith, didn't I tell ya Annie can cook real good?" Mark said proudly.

"You sure did, son."

Cane, Annie and Callahan looked at each other before bursting into laughter.

"What's so funny?" Mark asked, confused.

"We're happy to have Mr. Smith share a meal with us. I'd say that's something to be happy about, wouldn't you?" Callahan replied.

"Sure is, and he's got black hair like me, too. How about that, Pa?"

The adults' humor dissipated at the innocent remark. Cane swore inside. Damn, telling Mark that he was his natural father wouldn't be easy for any of them.

The meal ended, and Cane and Mark went off to the library to play checkers.

~ * ~

Her father finished his coffee. "Cane's willing to take things slow, honey."

19

Tears filled her eyes. "That's one good thing."

"Do you know the man just got out of prison, after serving seven years?"

Annie gasped. "Oh, my heavens! Is he…I mean…is he danger...?"

"He'd been unjustly accused of a train robbery. Judge Hopkins re-opened the case recently upon new evidence that cleared Cane of all charges. He's a good man, Annie, and you know it."

She nodded. "I know he is. I feel it in my heart. How awful that he's lost so much of his life though."

"Yes, and he means to atone for those lost years by making a life for him and Mark. He's planning on staying in the Bozeman area, and starting up his own ranch."

"Oh! That's wonderful."

Callahan eyed his daughter. "You know, Annie, I think I've hit upon a solution to this problem."

She frowned as she rose. "What would that be?"

"You could marry him."

"Father! You can't be serious."

"But I am. As I said, I've a good feeling about him."

"I think you're right. My instincts tell me he's good and he's suffered too much in life, but I can't marry him. We barely know each other. Not to mention the fact he hasn't asked me, and likely won't."

And until I discover the identity of the man from my last vision, I can't think of Cane Smith as anything but my enemy.

"Just thought this would remedy the situation is all."

"Once he learns about my queerness, I don't think he'll want me for a wife."

He grinned. "You never know, honey. It might be the very thing that attracts him."

She scoffed, "You dreamer you."

He left the kitchen, and she turned back to her work. The few men who'd come a-courtin' ended their interest real fast once they heard the talk in town about her gift of "sight." People were spooked about her abilities, even those who'd known her all her life, with the exception of a few people. Her father, of course, and Katie and James Freeman. She couldn't change who she was, what she was. Maybe someday, some man

20

would appreciate her gift and not think was crazy.

As she cleared the table, her mind raced at the idea of marrying Cane. She *could* marry him. It would solve all of their problems. Mark would have parents and a familiar home, too, and they wouldn't have to move away. They would live in the Bozeman area, close to her father.

She thought about the handsome, cool Cane Smith and shook her head. How could she be considering this? She could never marry him. The man was a tortured soul. More than once, she'd seen the sadness in his dark eyes. She didn't trust him, and wouldn't—until her premonition came to fruition one way or another.

Maybe the vision was meant as simply a forewarning that Cane was coming to claim his son, and nothing more. She shook her head.

No.

The premonition held nothing but evil. She decided Cane wasn't the man in the vision. She didn't know him well but, like her father, knew instinctively he was a good man.

As she lay in her bed that night, she was stunned when the premonition played in her mind again. She'd never had the same vision more than once. What could this mean? More importantly, who was the man who yanked Mark from her arms?

~ * ~

The following morning, Annie was the first to rise. She started breakfast, knowing soon her father, Mr. Smith, and Mark would be up and about. Her father would supervise the work on the ranch as he did every day. Annie was scheduled to work at The Palace. Mark would accompany her, as usual. He played well with Melanie while the adults worked.

She wasn't prepared for Cane to saunter into the kitchen first, clean-shaven, hair still wet and combed back from his forehead. He wore a pair of clean dungarees and a chambray shirt. She noticed how broad he was across the chest, how long and powerful his frame.

He cleared his throat. "'Mornin'," he said.

"Good morning," she replied before turning back to the flapjacks. Why was her voice so unsteady? Darn the man for being so handsome.

You need a beau, Annie Callahan, that's the problem.

"There's bacon, toast and beef hash on the table if you'd like to start

21

while I finish cooking the cakes. Coffee's there, too."

"Anything I can do to help?"

Annie shot him a glance and saw he was serious.

Bless the man.

She couldn't recall if her father had ever offered to help with household chores. The Lord said woman was helpmate to man. She smiled, thinking of Cane's offer in reverse. Mr. Cane Smith was looking more and more attractive.

As she watched him reach up to the shelf for a coffee cup, she said, "You're our guest, Mr. Smith, so just sit down and eat."

She heard a chair scrape across the floor. All the while, as she poured the batter and flipped the cakes, she felt his gaze on her—his intense gaze. For once she was glad of her gifts. An unexpected chill raced through her then and she frowned. Nervous as a polecat in a room full of rocking chairs, she finished cooking.

Annie forked several pancakes onto Cane's plate. He moved so quickly to allow her elbow room, he nearly tipped his chair back. She jammed her free hand down on the back of it and tipped him forward until all four legs settled on the floor.

"Thank you, ma'am," he muttered.

The loud, sharp sound of shoe-clad feet running down the old rickety stairway that led into the kitchen made Katie scowl. Mark opened the door at the bottom and ran to the table, sinking into his seat. "Smells good, Annie!"

"Haven't I told you not to use those stairs?"

"Sorry, but I'm hungry and they're closer."

"Next time you won't get any breakfast if you use them. They're dangerous. Understand?"

"Yes, ma'am. When we gonna fix those stairs?" he grumbled.

She sighed. "Hopefully sometime this winter."

Moving to her own chair, her thoughts returned to Cane. She wondered why he was so flustered around her. She was unused to men being self-conscious with her. Usually, it was the other way around.

She didn't ponder the idea long when Mark piped up, "Flapjacks! Yippee! My favorite."

Annie gave him a mock scowl. "Did you wash up first before you came to the table?"

"I sure did, and Pa will tell you so," Mark said self-righteously.

"He did," her father said as he entered the kitchen. He nodded at Cane. "Hope you slept okay, Mr. Smith."

"Call me Cane, please."

"Cane, then."

"I slept better than I have in seven years."

~ * ~

Silence ensued as Callahan and Annie stared at Cane. He didn't want their pity, but he saw it in their eyes. His jaw tightened instinctively.

"Uh, Mr. Smith?"

Cane looked at his son. "Yes, Mark?"

"You better get yourself a new bed if you haven't been sleeping so good."

Cane raised his brow. "You may be right."

Mark tilted his head to the side and stared at him for a long while. Eventually, he said, "How come you always call me 'son' like Pa does?"

Have I been calling him that? He cleared his throat. "No reason," he replied. Taking a sip of coffee, he glanced at Annie who sat across from him, her eyes filled with tears.

Damn!

He didn't want to make her cry.

Cane ate quickly, rose and moved to the sink where he washed his plate and coffee cup in the soapy water, then rinsed it in a second pan of clear, hot water. Leaving the dishes on the sideboard to dry, he looked at Annie. "Excuse me. I'll hitch up your wagon, ma'am."

"Thank you."

Callahan said, "After Mark and Annie leave for the day, can you meet me in the library?"

Cane nodded, then strode outside, breathing in deeply of Montana's fresh air. If anyone asked him what he missed most in life, it would be years of lost liberty.

He hitched up the horse and wagon, and then took a seat on a wooden rocking chair on the porch. The chair creaked as he started rocking. Cane frowned, deciding he better stop before he broke it. When he pushed himself to his feet, Annie came outside.

"Sit. Rock. You won't break it. It's always squeaked," she informed him.

Cane raised his brow, thinking the woman was a mind reader! "I could fix that squeak for you, ma'am."

"Don't you dare. We like the chair, squeak and all. Father is waiting for you in the library."

He watched her head for the wagon, then followed her. Once he caught up with her, he placed his hands around her waist and eased her up onto the seat. She scowled down at him, picking up the leads. "Would you please stop sneaking up on me like that?" she scolded.

"Sorry." His lips quirked up into a half smile. "Just wanted to help."

She narrowed her eyes on him and he looked away, afraid he'd burst out in laughter. The situation wasn't all that funny, but he hadn't felt this carefree—free—in years.

"I don't mind the help, but let me know somehow you'll be helping," she said.

"Will do," he murmured. It seemed he could do little right around this woman but he admitted to himself he enjoyed her skittishness around him. It meant she felt something…for him. Then he thought, *Nah!*

She sighed. "Sorry. I'm just crabby because I believe I should be part of this discussion, but it seems I won't be."

Cane nodded, understanding her shortness now.

Mark tore out of the house. Scrambling up onto the seat beside Annie, he said, "Bye, Mr. Smith!"

Annie snapped the reins, encouraging the horse on its way. "Good day to you, Mr. Smith," she called.

He watched her expertly handle the horse and wagon until it disappeared from sight. Annie Callahan was too independent, he decided, scowling. No woman of his would go off in a wagon by herself. Plenty of danger lurked on the roads.

Inside the library, he sat with another cup of coffee. Together, he and Callahan planned how to break the news of Mark's parentage to him.

"I say we just sit him down and tell him," Cane said.

By the look on Callahan's face, he knew the man would argue the point.

"We can't just blurt out the fact you're Mark's father without some preparation."

"Then what do you suggest? I've lost time in life and need to get on with it. I can't move ahead and make plans for my life until Mark's told."

"You say you plan on staying here, right?"

Cane nodded. "Soon as I can find myself a spread."

"Money is no object?"

Suspiciously, Cane murmured, "Pardon me for saying so, sir, but that's my business."

Damn the man for making him feel inferior. He'd managed to save quite a sum of money from his cattle-driving days, with plans then to return for Giselle, Mark's mother. Upon his arrest, the money had been taken from him by Texas law enforcers, who believed it to be evidence— money that'd been stolen in the train robbery. When Cane was released from prison, they'd returned his money to him, with interest.

"You're right. I apologize," Callahan said. "How about this arrangement? Stay and work for me for a while so Mark can see you every day. During that time, he'll get used to you and the two of you can bond naturally. Instead of Annie taking Mark with her to The Palace when she works, you can take him along with you on ranch jobs here. Oh, and I pay my hands well."

Cane had to admit it was a reasonable plan. Steady money coming in was even better.

Callahan added, "I won't charge you boarding fees while you work for me either."

"How long?" Cane asked.

"For as long as it takes Mark to form an attachment to you."

"We have no idea how long that will be."

Callahan sighed as he leaned back in his chair. "We've never talked with Mark about his past. He's never asked, though, as I mentioned earlier, we did tell him he'd been adopted. We'll begin telling him now, in bits and pieces."

"All right."

"You know, you deciding to stay around here will help ease the changes the boy will be facing."

"I don't think I'd want Mark to live completely without the people

25

who've raised him. The people who love him."

"Actually, I was thinking about my daughter's attachment to Mark, and not the other way around." Callahan frowned. "It'll be difficult for her."

"Uh, pardon my rudeness in saying this," Cane said, "but how come she hasn't married yet?"

Callahan narrowed his eyes on Cane. "You're new to town and haven't heard anything about my daughter, have you?"

"Nope, haven't really spoken with anyone but the judge, you and her, and Mr. and Mrs. Freeman, when I first arrived in town."

"Annie has a rather unusual gift."

The tactful way the man spoke immediately made Cane wary. "What do you mean?"

"She can see things others can't, future events, in particular."

One of the books passed onto Cane in jail had been the story of a man who had second sight—the ability to see things in his mind others couldn't, especially things in the future that hadn't occurred yet. He'd been skeptical. "I don't believe in all that crap."

"Most people don't. I didn't myself when Annie was just a girl—thought she was pretending. She was eight years old, very young at the time when I first noticed how different she was."

"Even if she does have this unusual ability, you can't deny the fact your daughter's a beautiful woman and should have found someone to marry by now."

"She is that, for certain. I'd love for her to marry and give me grandchildren, but no one's asked her yet. Maybe someday someone will. Jed Porter, a rancher nearby, has made overtures of late. She isn't all that old. Just twenty-two."

Cane thought twenty-two was plenty old enough to marry. Heck, he knew women who'd married at fourteen. "Well then, claiming Mark may help your daughter see that she should get married and start her own family. I suspect Mark fills that void in her life right now."

"You're right about that." Callahan rose and stretched out his hand. "Are we in agreement then that we'll ease Mark and Annie into these changes?"

Cane stood and took the older man's hand. "Agreed. It's October now, so I'd like to have Mark with me by Christmas, in our own place."

"Then you'd better start looking at some property while you're staying here. I suspect you'll want to find a place with a house on it since you won't have time to build one."

"That's right."

Callahan opened a desk drawer and pulled out a folded newspaper. "Here's the *Bozeman Herald*. It comes out three times a week. Folks list their properties for sale. Go ahead and check out some of these places."

"Thanks, Callahan."

"Thank *you*, Cane, for giving our family the time we need to adjust."

Cane left the library, detouring to the kitchen to refill his coffee. Sinking into the creaky rocking chair on the porch, he quickly scanned the property ads. He circled those that interested him, tucked the newspaper between spokes of the porch railing, and thought about Annie.

Second sight. Even after reading a book about the reality of this phenomenon, I can't get myself to believe it.

He leaned back in the chair and closed his eyes. Strange, unexpected things happened in life all the time. Whether he believed in her abilities or not, it didn't matter to him. But then, if she did have this particular gift of seeing things in the future, it might come in handy sometime.

Chapter Three

With the loan of a horse from Callahan, Cane spent the day looking at two ranches. The properties, separated by other ranches, were too small in acreage for raising cows and horses.

Then he rode the ten miles back to Bozeman to check out what folks in town had to offer by way of horseflesh. After looking at several for sale, he decided the horse he'd ridden in was better than any he'd seen and decided to make Callahan an offer. He returned to the Moonstruck Ranch, arriving just as Mark and Annie drove their wagon into the drive.

Mark jumped down and ran into the house. Raising his arms to assist Annie, Cane lowered them when she just stood there, one hand braced on the back of the seat.

"You too independent to accept a man's help?"

Damn. I didn't mean to sound so self-defensive. Seven years in prison will do that to man.

She stared at him a long moment before she let go of the seat and leaned forward, reaching for his shoulders. His hands spanned her waist, and he eased her down to the ground. She *was* too independent for her own good. Surely, she had to see that herself.

She smiled and shrugged her shoulders. "Perhaps."

"If I were your pa, I sure wouldn't allow you to drive that wagon all by yourself the way you do. It's not safe for you or Mark."

"I've been driving myself all my life. Nothing has ever happened to me."

"There's always a first time. It's not just your safety I'm thinking of, but Mark's. I want someone to drive you."

28

She laughed mirthlessly. "Who, for instance?"

Cane scowled. "Your pa's got plenty of ranch hands. He could spare one of them the short trips to and from town."

"All right. Since you've no employment or ranch to run, Mr. Smith, *you* may drive us."

He nodded. "Now you're being sensible."

She gaped at him.

He smiled. She'd expected him to refuse.

Pivoting on her heel, she huffed into the house.

Cane looked after her with a smile. While he'd been out looking at properties, every time he pictured Mark in his life, he pictured Annie, too, as if the two were a packaged deal. Home, family and work all appealed to him. If he married Annie, the boy would have parents and a loving grandfather, too. Marrying Annie would be the right thing to do for Mark.

That wasn't the only reason, of course. He could take care of her, protect her. In time, they would grow to love each other. He had better hurry, too, if the neighboring rancher had his sights on Annie. First, he'd talk to her father and get his blessing and... But what if Callahan didn't give it? What man in his right mind *would* want his daughter to marry a man who'd done time?

Damn, I was innocent! Maybe I'm the only person in the world to believe it, but I'm as good as the next decent man. Somehow, I have to lay to rest any doubts Callahan and his lovely daughter have about me. How can I prove myself?

Inside the house, he found Annie cooking again.

"Cook still sick?" he asked.

"Mrs. Williams is still ill, and now her mother, as well. She quit permanently to care for her." She eyed him up and down when he rolled up his sleeves and washed his hands. She still stared at him when he glanced back at her. Cane felt something then—a pleasant awareness of her beside him as she cooked up slabs of ham. Potatoes and a pot of greens boiled on the stove. Biscuits turned golden brown in the oven.

He found her grinning as he dried his hands on his thighs. Looking down at his wrinkled, stained shirt, self-consciousness set in.

"What's so funny?" he said.

"You've two missing buttons. Do you know where they are?"

29

He shook his head. "Long gone, I suspect. These are the clothes they gave me when I left prison. Hand-me-downs. And call me Cane."

She nodded. "I've extras, Cane. After supper, give me your shirt and I'll sew them on."

"Just hand over needle and thread, ma'am, and I can do it."

One silken brow lifted. "Annie, please. You can?" At his nod, she added, "I don't mind."

He smiled. "Sounds good. My mother used to do it."

"Where is your mother?"

"She met a Canadian who'd come down to work as a cowboy back home in Texas. When he'd made the money he needed to buy his own spread, he set himself to buy a place back home. He and my mom married, then she left with him."

"And your father?"

"Never knew him."

"Oh, sorry."

Tom Callahan arrived home with two of his hands, their neighbor, Jed Porter, and the circuit judge, Simon Hopkins. Callahan was lucky his daughter had cooked enough food since Cane knew, by the surprised look on her face, she hadn't been expecting company.

Cane sat down next to the judge, then shook his hand, knowing they'd already had this conversation when Cane got into Bozeman. "I can't thank you enough for all of your help, Judge Hopkins."

"If there was ever a man who didn't belong in prison, it was you," said Hopkins. "I've always been a fair judge of people, and I had a gut feeling you were innocent. Sorry that it took so long to prove it though."

"What's all this about?" Porter asked his eyes narrowed on Cane.

Hopkins explained Cane's predicament, including being sent to jail for a crime he didn't commit. Afterwards, Jed sent unsettling looks at Cane. Cane stared the man down, silently daring him to make some snide comment. He knew of men like Porter—privileged, tough, unfair and unkind to humanity in general.

During dinner, Cane decided Porter was showing too much interest in Annie. If the cowboy said one wrong word to her, he'd toss him out on his ear.

She wasn't a flirtatious woman, but she was a beauty with long, wheat colored hair bundled up at the back of her neck and pretty blue eyes. She was petite—he'd noticed when he'd helped her up and down out of the wagon—and her laughter was contagious. He found himself grinning whenever she laughed.

"So, what brings you here, Jed?" Annie asked.

He gave her a devilish grin that made Cane see red. "Just bought a few horses from your pa and he invited me to stay. Glad I did."

Mark finished eating and fidgeted in his chair. Cane took pity on him. "How about some checkers, Mark?"

"You bet!" Mark's face lit up brighter than a full moon on a clear, starry night.

"Excuse us?" Cane said. At Annie's nod, he looked at Mark. "Come on, son."

Cane tried concentrating on the game but found his attention drifting toward Annie's laughter in the kitchen. With the library door open, he heard nearly every word of conversation. Then he heard Porter murmur, "Come set out on the porch with me, sweet Annie."

Once again, he heard her girlish laughter and grimaced.

"You got a stomachache, Mr. Smith?"

Cane met Mark's inquisitive expression. "No. Why?"

"Your eyes are all squinty, and you got a frown on your face. You look like you got a stomachache."

"I don't. I'm just thinking about something that doesn't agree with me."

Like Annie sitting out on the porch with Porter. Sounds too much like courtin' to me. I should be the one on the porch with her.

Tonight, after the company left, he decided he'd speak with Callahan. If he got a blessing, he'd propose to Miss Annie—hopefully by tomorrow. What would her answer be?

Cane looked across the table at his son. Maybe she'd accept his proposal before any other man's because he was Mark's father.

~ * ~

"Jed, I said no for the second time." Annie scowled up into the frustrated face of her neighbor and would-be suitor.

"Why won't you marry me, Annie? What did I ever do wrong?"

31

"Nothing." She sighed. "Nothing at all. Simply put, I appreciate our friendship, but marriage? No, it wouldn't be right. I've no romantic inclinations toward you, Jed. Now don't ask me again."

They sat in chairs on the front porch, having a discussion Annie did not want to have.

Her stomach somersaulted in dread when, as the sun set, she caught Jed's face in profile. Everything about him was familiar to her, but something else stirred inside her. She'd seen that profile in anger before, his set jaw. At the same time, he looked at her again, she realized it.

The premonition! Jed is the man in my vision. No! It can't be. He'd never harm me or Mark. He's always been a perfect gentleman. He's helped us in so many ways over the years.

She scampered up from her chair. "Good night, Jed." She swiftly entered the house, ignoring his protests.

Detouring into the library, she found both Cane and Mark bent over the checkerboard concentrating. She sat down on the divan. From a wicker basket beside her, she picked up a wool sock to mend.

Smiling, she watched the two, thinking how they'd assumed the same hunched over position, elbows on their knees as they studied the checkerboard.

"Mind if I join you?" she softly asked.

~ * ~

Cane looked up. "Not at all." He glanced at Mark. "Hang on a minute, pardner." Rising to his feet he slowly unbuttoned his shirt, his eyes focused on Annie.

Interesting. She looked shocked, which made him hesitate, but only for a second. Her eyes were half closed and focused on his chest. He saw her sniff, her nostrils flaring a bit, as if catching his scent. It took him a second to remember what that look meant—it had been so long. Arousal—gut wrenching, body drenching, hot between the legs arousal—was the look on her face.

"What are you doing, Cane?" she whispered, dropping the sock to the floor.

Mark looked at Cane. "Looks like he's getting ready to turn in, don't it? Cane, you promised to finish the game," he protested.

"I will, while your sister sews the missing buttons on my shirt."

Cane shrugged out of the slightly tight shirt and held it out to her. She snatched it from him and dug around in the sewing basket on the floor. He sank into his seat to finish the game with Mark, conscious of her eyes on his bare back. Damn! It felt good to know she was attracted to him.

He made his move on the checkerboard, then looked at Annie again, watched her swiftly thread a needle with blue thread that was a fair match to his shirt. She picked up a white button from a small basket and sewed it on, chattering, "Father went to bed early with a headache. He gets them occasionally..."

She picked up the second button and quickly sewed that on the shirt, too. She bit the thread between her teeth and tossed Cane his shirt. "There. All done."

"Sis? Somethin' wrong?" Mark asked.

Her head shot up. "What do you mean?" Her gaze left Mark and moved to Cane who had donned his shirt, still sitting in his chair, his back to her.

"Uh, maybe you need to have your eyes looked at by Doc. You sewed 'em on crooked, Annie."

Cane swiveled around to face her, a slow smile forming on his lips.

Annie glanced down at her work and sighed.

"That's okay," Cane said. "As long as there are buttons sewed on, I don't care if they don't line up so well with the buttonholes."

He watched her face turn an interesting shade of pink before she bent to pick up the sock she'd dropped earlier. He swiveled around to continue the game. Then he thought about Jed Porter. Casually, he said, "Something happen out on the porch?"

It took her almost a minute to reply he noticed.

"Why do you think anything happened?"

"You seemed fidgety when you first came in from the porch. I heard it in your voice. And you were talking real fast."

"Jed Porter proposed to me."

Cane froze. *Hell, did she accept? Am I too damned late to ask her myself?*

Cane released his breath. "I passed by his ranch today. It's quite a place. He appears to be doing real well for himself."

"Jed never dirties his hands with ranch work. His hired hands do it. He inherited the ranch from his father, who did all of the initial back-breaking work."

He looked over his shoulder at her. "So did you accept his proposal?"

"Of course not!" She scowled at him. "We grew up together. It would be like marrying kin."

One up for me.

"Uh, Cane, it's your turn," Mark said.

He shook his head and continued playing checkers with his son. After a while, Mark's head dropped to his chin.

"Mark?" Cane said softly, not wanting to startle the boy.

Mark started anyway and rubbed his eyes.

"Time for bed, Mark," Annie said. She dropped the sock into the basket beside her and rose to her feet. "I'll help you get ready."

"I will, too," Cane said.

Mark gave Cane a curious, sleepy look. "You gonna tuck me in?"

"If you want me to, I will."

"Annie always reads to me first."

Cane nodded. "I can do that."

Mark gave Annie a kiss good night. Cane saw sadness—and resignation in her eyes. It'd begun. She seemed to accept that it was time for him to be Mark's father—for Mark to become a Smith and not a Callahan.

Mark took Cane's hand and they went upstairs. Cane could hardly breathe, so sweet and innocent was his son's gesture. The boy trusted him. Cane's eyes smarted.

He read from *Tom Sawyer*, until Mark fell asleep. Then Cane made his way down the stairs and back to the library, intent on asking her to be his wife, now, instead of waiting to talk to her father. Now, before he lost his courage.

He found her sitting on a window ledge seat, staring out into the night. He went to her, and she rose from the seat as though expecting a confrontation. Then she astonished him when she threw herself against his chest and he took her into his arms.

Holding her against him, he heard her sobs. She cried against his shirtfront until it was wet and clammy. Eventually, she said, "I can't let him go, Cane. I just can't."

Cane took her shoulders and stepped back from her.

Now or never.

With a trembling finger, he traced a tear down the porcelain slope of one cheek and slowly said, "Maybe you won't have to, Annie."

~ * ~

She raised her brows in amazement. Had he changed his mind about claiming Mark? Searching the gentle expression in his eyes, she looked up at him in confusion, her legs feeling numb, and then she sank to her seat. "I don't understand," she whispered.

"I meant what I said. You won't have to give up Mark…if you marry me."

Hope and joy soared through Annie. My heavens, she felt giddy at the thought of marrying Cane. Astonished at the idea of his asking for her hand in marriage, she paused, then frowned. But *had* he asked her?

No, he hadn't proposed, not really. Not in the way she believed a man should propose to a woman. She bit her lip, deep in thought, then straightened her shoulders, deciding it was a proposal, albeit not a traditional one, but still a proposal. "Why are you asking me to be your wife?"

"You want Mark in your life, don't you?"

"Of course I do. More than anything, but marriage is a drastic step. We're all but strangers, Cane."

He bent down and pressed firm lips against hers. They lulled her, made her want him more than she'd ever wanted a man before. She sighed against his lips, then turned her head, breaking the kiss.

"We'll grow to know each other, love each other." Taking her hands, he pulled her to her feet and slid his hands around her waist.

Though she found she enjoyed his masculine size and warmth, Annie pressed her hands against his chest to make contact with his gaze.

"You're right. Over time, we'll learn to care for each other. But at first I'd need time to…" She couldn't meet his eyes, embarrassed yet thrilled at the thought of sharing the same bed with him.

"You can have all the time you need to get used to me. Hopefully, it won't take you too long to decide you like me enough to make ours a true

35

marriage. Say yes, Annie," he encouraged her. "Then we can get your father's blessing."

"Wait. I need to tell you about me, something important."

"You mean the visions? Your father already did."

Astonished, she widened her eyes. My God, he'd asked her to marry him, even knowing about her unusual gift. "Well...well...how do you feel about that? About me?"

"Nothing to be ashamed of."

"A gift, yes, if you can call it that. It took me years to get used to it. I've had a recent premonition, one that's alarming to say the least, and it's occurred three times. This has never happened to me so often before—the same vision."

He pressed down on her shoulders until she sank to the window seat once more. Sitting beside her, he again took her hands in his. "Tell me what you saw."

She sobbed and tears filled her eyes. "A man trying to take Mark from me."

"When did you have this vision?"

She sniffled. "Moments before you walked up to my wagon at the schoolhouse."

"What you saw was me claiming Mark."

Annie shook her head. "No. It wasn't you. It was another man. I believe it was Jed. He tore Mark from my arms. I can still hear Mark's screams."

"Then what happened?"

"The premonition stopped. I've no idea what happens after that."

Cane stroked her cheek, helping her trembling abate slightly. "Don't worry. I'm here to protect both of you. No one will dare take Mark from us."

She smiled at him and nodded.

"I'm asking again, Annie. Will you marry me?"

Tears filled her eyes even as she whispered, "Yes."

He raised his brow. "You mean it?"

"This is a sensible solution to this dilemma, not to mention the fact that it'll be so much easier for Mark."

"Is that your only reason for saying yes?"

36

"Isn't it the only reason you asked me?"

She looked into his eyes and caught a glimmer of disappointment. She had to be truthful with him. While she was attracted to him, she didn't love him. She believed that love would come to them over time, as they grew to know each other.

He dragged his fingers through his hair. "I was hoping for... Never mind. When do you want to get married?"

~ * ~

Damn! So much for romance. So she doesn't love me. What did I expect? We've known each other only two days, yet I half convinced myself I was already falling in love with her. But then, a lot has happened in these two days.

"I think we owe it to Mark to get to know each other better before we marry. Perhaps in a few months we can say our vows."

"Sounds sensible," Cane said.

"When will you talk to Father about us?"

"As soon as I can." Cane turned on his heel and headed toward the door.

"Where are you going?"

He came to a halt and quirked an eyebrow at her. "Turning in for the night. I've got a big day ahead of me and several properties to look at. I'm rising before the sun. Good night."

"Yes, good night, Cane," she said faintly.

After he left, she took up her darning again, joy bubbling up inside her. He'd asked her to marry him. Mark would be secure, and she'd still have the boy who was like a son to her in her life.

She hadn't missed the disappointment on Cane's face and guessed he'd expected her to declare her love for him. He hadn't declared his love for her either. She greatly admired Cane's strength and determination to make something of his life. His love for Mark was genuine. Though convinced she would grow to love him, she harbored doubts about him falling in love with her. His purpose in life had been to gain the custody and love of his son. He would achieve that goal with their marriage. Was that his only reason for proposing?

It would be enough, she decided, though she hated the idea. She

37

finished darning the sock and tossed it into a basket. She thought about Cane's dark hair and eyes, his swarthy complexion and strong body when he'd pulled her against him.

Love made no difference to a man who'd lived without love for most of his life, a man with the single-minded purpose he'd had in coming here. Love mattered to Annie, enough to make her determined to be such a good wife to Cane, he would have no choice but to fall madly in love with her. She would show him the difference love could make in his hard life.

Chapter Four

After a few days of living with the Callahans, Cane's desire to marry Annie and take her to his bed had grown faster than a brush fire. It was all he could think about—holding her sweet body in his arms, taking down her wheat-colored strands of hair, planting his lips against hers. He was going insane with wanting her! Yet he knew he had to wait. He'd give her the time she needed to get used to him. He'd promised.

He'd had no luck finding property on which to build a ranch and a home for Annie and Mark. It had to be the right property. With the approaching winter, he knew he was running out of time, too. He was weary and somewhat discouraged as he rode into town, cold and hungry. For the past hour, he'd been looking forward to enjoying a meal. There was Annie's wagon outside Katie's Palace. *Darn it! Didn't I tell the woman I didn't want her driving by herself?*

His stomach rumbled when he smelled beefsteaks. He swung off his horse, tied him up and ambled into The Palace. Removing his gloves, he welcomed the heat as he stood in the entryway and looked around. With a quick sweep, he decided there was no vacant table. Then his gaze honed in on Annie. She was setting a table at the opposite end of the restaurant. She turned, smiled, and motioned him back.

He pulled off his Stetson. She looked pretty in a russet-colored dress embellished with ivory lace. He was nothing but a hard cowboy who'd seen and experienced too much pain and violence in life, yet her femininity intrigued and enticed him—softened him.

He strode to the table she'd just cleaned up. She pulled a chair out for him and waited for him to take it. As he sat, he said, "You sure are a sight

39

for these tired eyes."

"Ah, your words are poetry to my ears, Cane."

Narrowing his gaze on her, he saw her sweet smile but knew her reply was anything but flippant. "Poetry, huh? That's the first time anyone has ever accused me of that. I read, but I'm no poet."

"All right, how about this then? You're just being nice to me so I'll keep sewing buttons on your shirt when you lose them."

"Yup, that's the size of it." He grinned at her. The woman knew how to put a man at ease. His chest expanded when she grinned back and tilted her head.

"You know, if you want I could sew you some new shirts."

Cane gulped down the lump forming in his throat. Outside of his mother, no woman had ever offered to do something so nice for him. He didn't know what to say to her offer. He just sat there like a dunderheaded fool, staring at her.

"No, thanks," he eventually managed to say, looking away. "I can't afford to spend a dime on clothing until I purchase my property and figure out how much I'll have left over for cattle and horses and gear."

"I've bolts of chambray and woolens at the ranch. You won't be the first man for whom I've made a shirt. Every hand on our ranch has had at least one made by me."

"Why?" he asked, even as jealousy tore through him at the thought of her hands measuring another man's body.

"I enjoy sewing, for one, and most of the men have never had anything done for them—certainly not a homemade shirt. I appreciate their work for us at the ranch, and one way I show my thanks is to make shirts for Christmas. Some of our hands have been with us since I was a girl. They're family to me." She clapped her hands and laughed. "Oh, you should see how we decorate the house for the holidays. The baking and cooking in preparation! And, on Christmas morning, the hands who have no other family open gifts with us and share a festive meal."

He nodded. "Then I look forward to you making me a shirt for Christmas, Miss Annie." *And sharing our first Christmas together, even if it's not as man and wife for I can't marry her without a home for her and Mark.*

She gave him a shy smile. "I...I have to get back to work. Would you like the special? It's beefsteak."

"Much appreciated, and coffee," he said. "Oh, and one more thing."

"What's that?"

"I'll be back in a couple hours to escort you home."

She frowned. "I don't have Mark with me, Cane. It's not necessary."

"Maybe not to you, but it is to me."

"Hey, Annie, our food's sitting up on the kitchen shelf getting cold!"

Cane looked beyond Annie to see Jed Porter glaring at him. "Go on. We'll talk later," he said.

Annie nodded and left him. He stared out the window, deciding there'd be plenty of time to ponder on how pretty Annie was once they were married. It wasn't long before he looked toward the kitchen and followed her activity as she delivered plates of food to one table then another. When she paused with her hands full at Jed's table, Cane's world turned red. Jed sat with two other men and, with a smirk on his lips, slid an arm around Annie's waist after she set his food down.

Cane scowled. Then he grinned when she whipped a wooden spoon from her apron pocket and smacked Jed's hand. Jed retaliated, wound his hand around her neck and yanked her down to meet his lips.

Cane rose from his chair with a vivid curse and tore down the aisle. Stopping beside Jed, Cane grasped the man's wrist and pulled his hand from around Annie's neck. "Let go of her," he growled.

Jed stumbled to his feet, knocking his chair over in the process, fists raised. "Who in the hell do you think you are?"

Cane maneuvered Annie behind him, conscious of the silence in the room, knowing now they had an audience. He took advantage of the quiet and said, "The man who will be marrying Miss Annie, that's who."

Jed glared at Annie. "Is that true?"

Annie nodded. "Yes."

"And don't propose to her again, either," Cane warned. He started to turn Annie away with him but paused, focusing on Jed again. "And one thing more, don't you ever lay a hand on her again. Understand?"

Jed didn't reply, just glared mulishly at Cane.

James Freeman entered The Palace. He eased up to them. "There a problem here?" he asked.

"Oh, James, why…"

41

"Not anymore," Cane inserted. "Porter here was just leaving. Weren't you?"

Jed sent smoldering looks at Cane and Annie, then curtly nodded. "Come on, boys."

Cane's gaze followed Jed and his men until they left the saloon, then he looked at Annie.

"I'm marrying Cane," Annie said. "Jed's not too happy about it."

"Is that right?" James replied with a grin.

Annie nodded.

The swinging kitchen doors opened as James said, "Bet you haven't told Katie yet, have you?"

"Told me what?" Katie asked, joining them.

"The two of them are getting married," James said. He wound an arm around Katie's expanding waist. "Ain't that something?"

"Oh, Annie! When were you going to tell me?" Katie said accusingly.

"It pretty much just happened, ma'am," Cane said. "We're getting married sometime around Christmas."

Annie's eyes went round. "We are?"

"Yes," Cane said decidedly. "By the way, I never did get my cup of coffee or my supper."

Katie laughed. "Sit down, Mr. Smith. Coming right up."

James stared at Cane a moment, then he stuck out his hand. "Hope you realize you're getting a real treasure with Annie."

"I do," Cane said and shook the marshal's hand.

Cane returned to his seat, glad folks were involved once again in their own table conversations.

Annie rushed up. "Here's your coffee, Cane. Supper should be up any moment."

"Thanks. No rush," he replied. "You okay?"

She nodded but wouldn't meet his eyes.

"Are you mad at me for making the announcement like I did?"

"No." She hesitated, biting her lip a moment before replying. "No one's ever stood up for me like you did. Thank you for that." She leaned down and planted a quick kiss on his cheek, surprising him.

He reached for her. "Annie, I…"

"I'll be back in a minute." She rushed to the kitchen. Within moments, she delivered his food, and he forced himself to eat slowly even though hunger gnawed at his belly.

Cane finished his meal, left money on the table, including a generous tip for Annie. Jamming his Stetson on his head, he paused at the door and caught Annie's eyes as she left the kitchen with a tray loaded with plates of food.

"I'll be back, like I said, to fetch you."

She nodded and delivered the food on the platters.

Uneasiness settled over him. He'd ride home on his horse, return in two hours, then escort her home in her wagon. As he mounted his horse, he smiled. *Home. I like the sound of that, especially coming from Annie.*

~ * ~

Annie was exhausted when she left The Palace at half past nine. As she neared the double doors, she heard the rain before she smelled it. Beside her, Katie said, "I can't thank you enough for coming in. I owe you. Again."

"You don't owe me a thing," Annie replied. She laid her hand on the big swell of Katie's belly. "Moving a lot, isn't he?"

Katie placed her hand over her friend's. "It might be a girl, you know, but you always say 'he.'"

"I think this baby is a boy."

Katie gasped. "Tell me, did you *see* something?"

Annie shivered, grateful that she hadn't had any more premonitions since Cane's arrival. "No, sorry, I've seen nothing about your baby, Katie. Consider that a good thing."

Katie nodded. "I'll soon know. Every time he moves, I have to rush to the...well, you know."

They laughed. Stepping outside, a light mist fell around them. Annie pulled her coat close around her. "Wouldn't you know it? I took the wagon that leaks today."

"I can always send you home in one of mine," Katie said. "Besides, it'll be nearly dark by the time you get home. I don't like the idea of you traveling on your own."

"I got here on my own and I can return the same way," Annie said firmly. Besides, Cane would be on the way soon, if he was true to his word.

"The roads aren't safe at night," Katie protested.

"They're not safe during the day, either." Annie smiled. "Don't worry about me. It's only fifteen minutes to home." She paused for an instant before blurting what she knew she'd have to, sooner or later, "I guess I should tell you this. Cane Smith is Mark's true father."

Katie gasped, "Oh my! So is that why you're marrying him?"

"At first I thought it was the reason. You have to admit it's the practical thing to do. It'll be easier for Mark, too, adjusting to Cane as his father."

"But you don't know the man!" Katie protested.

"True, but I've good instincts, you can't deny. I've a feeling our marriage will be good, Katie. I feel things for Cane I've never felt for any man." Heat seeped into her cheeks. "Stirrings, I guess you'd say."

Katie nodded. "I know all about stirrings," she said, patting her stomach. "But, like I said, you don't know him. Maybe we should have James check up on him. What if he's some criminal?"

"As a matter of fact, he spent seven years in prison for a crime he didn't commit. He was released when the law found the real criminal."

"How horrible for him. But…do you want me to ask James to check out his past? Just to be on the safe side?"

"No. I believe every word he told me. Besides, Father spoke with Judge Hopkins, who verified Cane's facts."

"I suppose there's no chance you happen to love him, do you?"

"How could I? We just met."

"Yes, but don't forget those stirrings," Katie said with a laugh. "I'm happy for you."

"Thanks, Katie. I have the feeling you'll be having that baby very soon. You send someone to let us know about the baby right away. Okay?"

"I will," Katie promised.

* * * *

It was half past nine and rain pounded the ground. It was time to go get Annie. As Cane rode, he was soaked to the skin within moments. Without the moon's light, he had difficulty staying on the road. He wondered how Annie managed traveling home evenings after working.

But then she'd grown up here, and knowing her horse, he likely knew the way even if she didn't guide him.

He saw lights shining from Katie's Palace up ahead. He slowed down as he drew nearer and saw the shadowy shape of a wagon stopped in the road. Squinting through the rain, he saw a riderless horse beside a wagon and a hitched horse. Chills prickled up his spine. Could it be Annie?

Damn! Didn't I tell her to wait for me? Now it seemed her wagon had broken down. It also appeared someone had stopped to help her.

A woman's scream rent the night and he recognized it as Annie's. "Hee yah!" Cane hollered, whipping his horse into a gallop. He saw Annie, her arms flailing, legs kicking as she screamed at the man who was manhandling her as he sat on the seat beside her. Even though he saw only the shape of a big man, Cane's mind blared, *Jed!* He leaned over his horse's neck and thundered toward them. Once he reached the wagon, he flung himself into it, snatching Jed up by the collar and whirling him away from Annie.

"You can't have her!" Jed yelled over the rain. "She's mine!"

His fist darted out and clipped Cane's chin. Cane staggered but regained his balance. Like a bull on the rampage, he butted his head into Jed's stomach, satisfied at the sound of the man's groan. Straightening, he pulled back his right arm and slammed his fist into Jed's face. Blood spurted from his nose. Jed gave a maddening roar and hauled back his own fist, but Cane hit him again and the brute tumbled out of the wagon.

Cane saw Jed lying sprawled in the mud, saw him twitch. Cane warned, "Stay put, if you know what's good for you." Then he took Annie in his arms, and she sobbed against his chest. "Are you okay?" he asked. At her nod, his voice hardened. "Didn't I tell you to stay put until I came for you?"

She looked up at him. "I grew up in Bozeman and had no reason to believe anything bad could happen to me. Heavens, I'd had no forewarning, no premonition, of Jed setting upon me like he did." But then she remembered her visions. Surely, Jed couldn't do this horrible thing.

She sighed. "It seems you were absolutely right about my safety."

"Finally, you see the sense of things."

She lifted her chin. "I've always been safe in Bozeman. This is my home, Cane. Though I have to admit I owe you thanks for arriving in so timely a fashion."

"Yes, if I hadn't arrived, who knows how far Porter would have gone?"

"Oh, I know exactly what he would have done. He...told me!" she said in a shaky murmur.

"What did he say?"

"He meant to ruin me so I'd have to marry him."

"The bastard!" Cane glared down at Jed, who still lay on the ground, groaning.

Suddenly, the marshal rode up, and Cane and Annie told him what had happened.

"You'll be spending the night in a jail cell, Porter," James muttered, hauling Jed to his feet. "You're lucky Miss Annie will let it go at that."

Time to head for home, Cane decided. He whistled, and his horse trotted over to him.

"You know, of course, Jed attacking me is all your fault, don't you?"

He had just grabbed his horse's reins when he whipped his head around to stare at her. "What!"

"If you had let me take care of things with him at The Palace, he wouldn't have come after me like he did."

Cane looped his horse's reins over one arm, then picked up the reins from the harnessed horse and snapped them against his flanks, setting him into a trot toward home.

"I think you're wrong on that, sweetheart. I think Porter had reached the end of his rope—even before he found out you were marrying me. Even if he hadn't discovered you accepted my proposal, he would have attacked you sooner or later, with the intentions of ruining you, hoping you'd have to marry him to save your reputation."

"Perhaps you have a point."

"You agreed to be my wife." Gentling his tone, he added, "You have to learn to trust my judgment, Annie."

He waited for her blast of fury, but was stunned when she said, "I do trust you, Cane."

"Good. I protect what's mine, and you belong to me. You can't deny it unless you plan on backing out of marrying me. Is that what you want?"

"No," she said softly.

He nodded. "Good. I'm glad we see eye to eye on this."

Annie sighed. "Perhaps, with time, you'll learn to trust our community and respect my desire for freedom to come and go as I please. As your wife, I'll obey you, but I don't want to be a prisoner."

She had to be joking. A beauty such as her couldn't be allowed to travel on her own without an escort, no matter that Bozeman was her hometown and she felt safe and knew everyone. Hopefully, with tonight's attack, she'd learned her lesson.

It was slow going through the mud, but soon they reached the drive leading to the house. He drove into the yard and stopped at the barn. A stable boy ran outside and unhitched the horse while Cane hustled Annie inside.

* * * *

"When I left this morning, I hadn't expected rain." She shed her coat and wrinkled her nose at the smell of wet wool. Cane took it and hung it up beside his own on pegs to dry.

"I imagine Father has retired already, hasn't he?"

Cane nodded.

"Darn! We need to talk to him about...our plans."

"We will tomorrow. Join me for a libation?"

"I'd love that, but I think we both need to change our clothes."

"Agreed," he said with a grin.

Cane was already at the foot of the stairs, waiting for her, after they'd gone to their rooms to change into dry clothing. He took her elbow and escorted her into the library.

As she sat on the divan before a crackling fire, she listened to Cane making their drinks. Soon, he sat beside her and handed her a cup. With her first taste, she knew he'd poured them hot coffee with a liberal dash of whiskey in it. Taking small sips, she relaxed and leaned back but startled when she felt something behind her neck.

"Sorry," he murmured.

She saw him lifting his arm, and she said, "Don't move. Your warmth is appreciated."

Heat suffused her cheeks when she saw the smile on his lips. Looking higher, she saw the passionate look in his eyes. He slid his arm over the

47

back again and pressed close to her. She sighed, loving the feel of him against her. Before long, she couldn't keep her eyes open as exhaustion overcame her.

* * * *

Cane grabbed her cup before she dropped it and set it down beside his on the table. He couldn't resist kissing her forehead, inhaling her lavender scent. His lips moved to the cheek near him. Her lips beckoned him, and he brushed his gently against the full curves of her own.

Dynamite exploded inside him, and he felt his body harden, readying for her—his woman. She woke slowly, turning her head toward him to kiss him back. Then she wound her arms around his neck and pulled him down further, returning his exploratory kiss.

When he felt ready to take her then and there, he came to his senses and eased her arms from around his neck. "Annie, we have to stop."

He smiled when she sighed in disappointment.

"I suppose you're right. Perhaps we should get married sooner."

His smile widened. "You won't find me objecting."

She nodded. "We'd better speak with Father first. He's always wanted me to get married in church, in a white dress, with flowers and a reception. I don't think we can plan something that elaborate so soon, but we'll see."

"The sooner the better," he said. His voice sounded raspy to him, and he couldn't resist kissing her again. She turned into his embrace. Cane couldn't help pulling her even harder against him, then his hand wandered higher, cupping one breast. He thought of the irony of telling her they had to stop when he couldn't, not when she was so willing in his arms.

"Ah!" she whispered when he raised her up from her seat and settled her on his lap, facing him. He palmed one of her breasts while the other stroked her lower back and bottom. Damn all the clothes women wore, he mused, wanting to strip her naked now, this moment, while the fire blazed high, his wanton desire for her just as hot.

"God, I want you," he murmured against her cheek. "Do you have any idea how long it's been since I've made love to a woman?"

Her laughter surprised him, and he looked down at her, his lips quirked. "That's funny?" he asked. At her nod, he added, "Not from where I'm sitting."

"For you it's been seven years." He noticed how her smile left then and tears filled her eyes. "For me it's been a lifetime."

He groaned. "Don't say that or I won't be able to stop."

"I don't want you to stop. Besides, what difference does it make? We are getting married, remember?"

He set her down beside him, then rose. Pacing in front of the fireplace, he said, "Yes, but I won't dishonor you, and I respect your father and how he's taken me in. We'll wait until our wedding night, and no complaints," he warned.

She pouted. "Have you always been so dictatorial?"

Had he? He thought a minute then grinned. "No. Never. Maybe this arrangement—this marriage between us—means more to me than I thought." He pulled her to her feet. "To bed with you now, sweetheart."

"All right. But I'd much rather stay here with you."

At the foot of the steps, he pulled her against him and kissed her until she went limp in his arms. "And I'd much rather you stayed here with me, too. See you in the morning."

Cane watched her ascend the stairs, her hips swinging. At the landing, she paused and smiled down at him, then blew him a kiss. "Good night, Cane."

Temptress! Scowling, he put one foot on the first step, ready to go after her when she swiftly disappeared down the hallway.

~ * ~

"No! No! Stop! You can't!"

Through Annie's closed bedroom door, Cane said calmly, "Annie, Annie, wake up. You're having a bad dream."

He heard her moaning, then a scream rent the air. Cane stood at the door, ready to open it when her father came charging from his room. Callahan opened the door and rushed inside. Cane saw Annie lying on her bed. Her eyes were tightly shut, and she was shaking her head wildly from side to side. Slowly, he moved into her room, his eyes steady on her.

"Annie, honey? Wake up," her father ordered as he bent over her and shook her shoulders.

Slowly, she quieted, then opened her eyes. Seeing her father, she sat up and threw herself into his arms.

49

"Another premonition?" her father asked as he held her.

Annie nodded. "It was awful. It was the same one, that man trying to take Mark away from me."

Cane's jaw tightened at her words, and he said, "As long as I'm living, no one will take Mark away from us. Go to sleep. You're safe. I won't let anything happen to either of you."

She looked up at him with sad but trusting eyes and nodded. "Good night. I'm sorry I woke everyone." She turned her back on them and closed her eyes.

In the hallway, Callahan said, "Come. Have a drink with me in the library."

"Good idea. I need to speak with you about something."

After they'd settled down with glasses of Irish whiskey, Cane tried to decide how to tell Callahan that he'd asked Annie to marry him and she'd agreed. True, he should have asked the old man's permission first, but getting Annie's agreement had seemed more urgent.

Finally, Cane came out with it. "I've asked Annie to marry me."

Callahan smiled and nodded. "Glad you're seeing things my way."

"I should have declared my intentions to you first, but—"

"Asking a father's permission was common in my day, but it seems to have slipped out of fashion. Thanks, though, for telling me, after the fact. I've always wanted to have a traditional wedding for her. She is my only child, after all, but I will understand if expediency is necessary for the two of you."

"It's true, for Mark's sake, we'd like to be married soon. I've yet to find a home for us though. Sure, there are plenty of properties, but they're all too small for my plans."

Sitting forward, Callahan said, "For a wedding gift, I'd like to give you and Annie sixteen-hundred acres of my property to the west."

"You don't have to do that," Cane protested, shocked.

Callahan shrugged. "I've wondered what would happen to the ranch once I've passed on, since I've no son. Truth be told, it was one of the reasons that made sense for me to adopt Mark. Naturally, Annie would get it, but I can't think of a better man to run this place than you, Cane, as my daughter's husband. Then you'll pass it onto Mark."

Cane gulped down the growing lump in his throat and nodded, staring down at the floor. "It's a mighty generous wedding gift, and we appreciate it."

Callahan nodded. "Someday it'll all be yours, Annie's and Mark's."

"Just how much land is there?"

Callahan just smiled. "We'd better get some shut-eye. We'll be up riding most of tomorrow. You'll get some idea of the acreage at that time."

"I'm up for it." Reaching out, Cane took Callahan's hand. "Thanks for giving me your blessing, and your daughter. I never believed I could get so lucky. Luck has not been my friend," he said dryly.

Callahan slapped his back in a friendly gesture, then left the library.

Cane sank down on the divan and stared into the fire. Closing his eyes, he thought back to when he'd been in prison and received the letter that would eventually change his destiny. Thank God, he'd never given up hope, for hope was what had helped him survive the remainder of his incarceration, while both he and the judge tried to prove his innocence. Now hope would give him a future.

Chapter Five

Cane spent the next four days riding the range with Annie's father, amazed by the acres and acres of land comprised of small lakes, streams, mountains and plains. The Moonstruck Ranch was like paradise to him, and it would soon be his home. Excitement flared deep inside him at the thought of building a house, of having Annie and Mark in his life permanently. And perhaps other children...

On Saturday morning, he found sticks to make fishing poles and string, then rode to The Katie's Palace to fetch Mark. Soon the streams and ponds would be frozen and fishing wouldn't be possible. He was intent on having a talk with the boy about marrying Annie. He'd discussed the plan last night with her and she'd agreed, as long as Cane didn't blurt out the fact that he was Mark's father. She wanted to be the one to decide when the time was right and now was too soon. She insisted they'd tell Mark *together*. Cane had reluctantly agreed.

As he rode, he started thinking of Christmas, somehow wanting to make this one special for Mark and Annie, and for himself. It'd been so long since he actually celebrated the holiday, he wasn't sure how or what to do, with the exception of purchasing gifts. He'd already decided on a fine pocketknife for Mark that he'd seen in the mercantile, even though he suspected Annie might not like the idea. Then there was Annie. He had no idea what to buy her for a present, except for one thing—a wedding ring.

As soon as he stopped outside The Palace, Mark came running out the front door.

"You taking me home instead of Annie?"

Leaning on his saddle's pommel, Cane said, "Thought we'd go over

52

to that pond near your house to do some fishing, before winter really sets in and it freezes over."

"Yes!"

"Go get your coat then."

Cane watched Mark run inside. His heart raced when Annie appeared in the doorway and smiled. Damn, she looked so pretty dressed in a modest blue gown that enhanced her fair complexion and matched her eyes. "You two have a good time."

"We sure will, Annie!" Mark said exuberantly as he squeezed past her.

Cane extended his hand to help him up on the horse in front of him. He tipped his hat to Annie. "See you at supper."

"Yes," she said, gave a little wave and went back inside.

As they rode down the street, Cane enjoyed the smell of little boy heat and dirt, feeling a stirring of love inside for this little man, sorry he'd missed so much of his life. He had plans to make up for the lost time.

For the rest of the day, the two of them fished, laughed, and talked. Finally, when Cane felt Mark was comfortable with him, he broached the marriage idea to him.

"What would you think if I married Annie?"

Mark frowned. "And take her away from Pa and me?" He shook his head. "I wouldn't like it."

"No," Cane quickly said, "I wouldn't be taking her away from you. Annie and I have decided we want to get married, and you'll come visit or even stay with us whenever you want."

"I can't leave Pa." Mark scowled. "But I don't want Annie to move away either. His eyes lit up then. "I know! You can live at our house," he offered.

Cane nodded. "For a while, while we build a house, we would. Your pa has given Annie and me some of his land on which to build our own home."

"Why can't you live with me, Pa and Annie? Our house is big!"

"It is, Mark, but it wouldn't be my home, and I need my own place real bad."

Mark thought about it and finally nodded. "Okay." Mark gave Cane a sad look. "I'm gonna miss seeing Annie every day."

53

"Count on seeing her every day, Mark. Things will still be the same."

Mark shrugged, then turned his attention back to his fishing pole. "Oh! I gotta bite! Look!"

Cane was thoughtful as he helped Mark pull in his fish. He'd promised Annie he wouldn't break the truth to the boy without her, but felt compelled now to do so. He opened his mouth, ready to ease into it, when he clamped it shut. A promise was a promise, and he wouldn't break it to Annie. He'd bide his time, until she felt Mark was ready to hear the news.

Mark whooped with joy when he saw his small fish. "Can we keep him?"

Cane grinned. "You know, son, he's a might small. I think he needs to go back into that pond. We'll try and catch a bigger one."

Disappointed, Mark said, "Okay, but he looks plenty big to me. I want to show Pa."

"We'll fish a bit more and see if we can catch one you can keep."

When it was long past time to leave the fishing hole, darkness had descended and the temperature had dropped. Unfortunately, Mark hadn't caught another fish.

"Time to go home," Cane said as he rose to his feet and brushed off his jeans.

Mark pouted as he scrambled up. "But I didn't get a fish!"

"You'll have a chance to try again soon."

"I don't wanna go home."

"Annie's probably home cooking supper."

"So can we come back tomorrow?"

"We'll see."

Mark's pout remained. "We *have* to."

Cane kept his patience, though he was somewhat surprised to see this petulant side of Mark. "I promised we'd fish again, and we will, though it might not be tomorrow."

Mark picked up his pole and trudged over to Cane's horse. Though Mark was quiet at the start of the trip home, Cane had him making plans for more fishing. He realized Mark had little concept of what tomorrow, or the day after tomorrow meant, yet, but he promised they'd go fishing sooner rather than later, while the weather held out, and the pond remained without ice.

~ * ~

Annie was cooking supper when they arrived home. She looked up when they entered the kitchen and smiled. "So, how was the fishing?"

"Not so good," Mark said his lower lip protruding.

Annie met Cane's eyes with a questioning look. "So, you didn't catch anything?"

"Cane wouldn't let me keep my fish."

"He was a small fry, that's why you couldn't keep him. I explained to you we'll go fishing again. Soon. I'm pretty sure you'll catch a bigger fish to keep next time."

"But I wanted that fish!"

"Mark," Annie began, but was interrupted when the boy stamped his foot and scowled at Cane.

Cane leaned down to Mark. "I made you a promise we'll go fishing again, but not if you can't accept my terms. You stop that fussing right now," he ordered.

Annie slid up to Mark and pulled him against her. She tucked her hand beneath his chin and saw the tears in his eyes. "What's this? Didn't you have a good time?"

"Yes," he said reluctantly. "Pa always lets me keep fish I catch, even the little ones."

"Well, I think you owe Cane an apology," she said. "He took time to take you fishing when he certainly didn't have to, and likely had other things to do.

Mark looked shyly up at Cane. "Sorry."

"That's okay, son."

Mark looked at Annie. "I'm hungry."

Annie smiled, flitted her gaze to Cane, whose expression looked sad. "We'll be ready in a couple minutes. Go upstairs and wash up now."

Mark trudged off. As he passed Cane, Cane reached out to touch his hair, but Mark shied away from him.

Cane sighed as he watched Mark leave the kitchen, then looked at Annie. "Guess I didn't make points today with him, did I?"

Annie came around the table and took his hand. "He does seem rather out of sorts. I'm surprised that you throwing back his fish set him off like that. Father's done the same thing several times. I'm thinking it's something else that's really upset him. Did you tell him we were getting married?"

"I did, but that's all." Cane frowned. "It didn't seem to really bother him, though he thought the best idea was for all of us to live here together."

"How did you reply to him?"

"I told him we'll be living here temporarily, until we build our own house. I explained how he could visit between the two houses." He raked his fingers through his hair. "You don't know how hard it was for me to keep his parentage a secret."

"I can imagine," she murmured. "Thanks for not telling him yet. Spend as much time as you can with him over the next few weeks and then we can tell him." She squeezed his hand.

Winding an arm around her waist, he murmured into her hair, "I want to tell him soon. And I want us to get married soon—real soon."

She tried pulling out of his embrace, but he wouldn't allow it. "Cane!" she said frantically, "Mark and Father will be here any minute."

"Set the date and I'll release you, sweetheart."

She nodded. "How about right before Christmas? That would give me time to make plans."

She heard Mark's running steps heading for the kitchen, and she pressed her hands against Canc's chest.

He let her go. "I guess I can wait that long. You know, of course, we'll have to live here until spring. With winter setting in, that's the soonest we can build a house."

"I know. It'll be harder for you than me, I'm afraid. This is the only home I've known."

"You and your father have been nothing but hospitable. It won't be a hardship living here until we build our house. You let me know what you'd like for our house—anything you want," he promised.

"Thank you," she said softly.

Cane prayed the next several weeks would pass quicker than a train at full speed.

* * * *

56

December arrived, and Bozeman and its inhabitants began preparing for Christmas, Cane noticed. Bozeman had also had its first snowfall a week ago, but most of it had melted since temperatures had climbed to spring-like numbers. The warmer weather encouraged the men in town to get the decorations up before the next cold spell, which would set in and last for several months.

Though Annie was in the midst of planning their wedding, she'd roped Cane into helping the marshal and others decorate the town. It had started snowing just as James and Cane finished their work. They headed inside Katie's Palace, welcoming a hot cup of coffee. Cane came to a dead stop when he saw Annie sitting in a chair, rocking the new Freeman addition. Luke James Freeman, born a week ago at a healthy nine pounds, was sobbing pitifully.

Cane saw Annie duck her head and hold the baby close, but he didn't stop fussing. She stopped rocking and jiggled the baby until the baby's father arrived.

"Thanks, Annie." James took his son in his arms. "I'll go fetch Katie. It appears Luke needs a bedtime snack."

He left, and Cane took his place beside Annie. "You ready to go home soon? By the way, where's Mark?"

"I'm ready, and Mark's at home with Father, helping pick out the Christmas tree—the biggest ever, he wants."

"Let's go home and see how he's doing." He took her arm.

Some men came stomping in then, and he turned to find Jed Porter and several of his hands. Porter sneered at Cane. It took all of Cane's fortitude to keep his hands from forming into fists and plastering the bastard's face. Again. Porter had been gossiping worse than any old woman in town about Annie lately. Cane had heard, from James, that Porter had accused Annie of being a witch. His hands formed into fists, and he took a step toward Porter but stopped when a hand grabbed his arm. Looking down, he saw Annie's worried expression.

She whispered, "He's nothing but a pest. He's just mad I accepted your proposal, not his."

Katie and James returned, their daughter Melanie with them, the baby in Katie's arms.

"Thanks so much for your help, Annie," Katie said.

"Yes, thank you," James said, holding onto Melanie. "Both of you."

"Any time," Cane murmured, settling Annie's arm through his.

Anne smiled. "You're welcome. See you all later."

As they made their way out of town, Annie kissed his cheek. Cane looked back and saw Jed Porter standing outside The Palace, scowling, his face beet red. Cane turned back to Annie with a satisfied expression.

Cane hoped the bastard would choke on his regret.

Chapter Six

December, 1888

One week before Cane and Annie's wedding, Montana was struck by a snowstorm. Ten inches of snow fell across the territory, blowing and drifting in the howling winds, closing down all businesses in town.

Tom Callahan had purchased several hundred head of Texas Longhorns from the abundance driven by cowboys from Texas to Montana that fall. Tom and Cane had set out mid-morning to call in the ranch hands and gather up as many of the herds as they could, hoping to save them from the blizzard.

Now Annie stood at the library windows, listening to the howling wind, watching the swirling snow. A horse appeared, then another, and she breathed a sigh of relief. More horses, stumbling along, fighting against the howling winds and driving snow, came into sight. Thank heavens they'd arrived home before dark.

"Mark! They're back!" she called.

"Yippee!" Mark shouted as he met up with her in the hallway. She followed Mark to the door. Mark yanked open the door and stepped back as a snow-covered mountain of a man plodded through the entrance.

"Cane?" Annie said, barely able to make out his features. He was covered in snow, ice pellets were frozen on his Stetson, a shadow of beard on his face. Her father stood beside Cane, looking years older than before he'd left the house. She'd insisted they wear long woolen scarves over their heads before putting on their hats. All she could think was how the scarves probably helped in saving them from freezing to death.

Shocked, Annie nevertheless took charge, grabbing both men's arms to guide them into the library. Her father sank to the divan and closed his eyes. "No. Stay awake, Father," Annie ordered. When he didn't respond but kept his eyes shut, she snapped, "Wake up!" She slapped him hard on one cheek, and he opened his eyes.

Glaring at her, he muttered, "What in the hell are you trying to do, woman? Kill me?"

None too gently, Annie pulled at his coat with Cane's assistance. "I won't have to kill you. You'll be doing it to yourself if you don't keep your eyes open. We need to get you warm before you can even think about sleeping."

Annie looked at Cane, who looked just as cold and tired. "Cane, let me help you undress." At his wolfish grin, she added, "Your coat only, you devil."

She eased his arms out of his coat sleeves. The woolen coat was soaking wet and stuck to his body. Annie peeled it from him until he stood in his damp shirt and soaking dungarees.

He sighed. "Need a hot bath, but first one for your father. I'll just sit by the fire once we take care of the ranch hands."

"Didn't they head on home?" Annie asked.

Cane shook his head. "Most of them live at The Palace. The weather's too bad to go to town now. They took up our offer to stay here in the barn."

"But we've no heat out there!" Annie protested. "How many came?"

Bundled in her winter-wear, Annie went to the barn with Cane. "Come inside the house, everyone," she called.

Hours later, after the last hand and her father had settled down for the night, Annie fell into a chair before the fire in the library. She and Cane sat and drank hot rum until they were sleepy-eyed. Cane stood up and swept his hair back from his forehead.

Annie stirred and sat up straight in her chair. "Sorry, I didn't mean to fall asleep on you like that."

He ambled over to where she sat and sank down on his haunches. She stilled when he reached up, took her face between his hands and kissed her. He murmured then against her lips, "You're exhausted. It's past our bedtime."

When he went to release her face, she clamped her hands over his. "I gave up both of our rooms tonight to others. This room is the only vacant one in the house. I want you to stay with me here for the night."

Cane groaned and closed his eyes. "You know we shouldn't. Not until we're married," he insisted.

She choked on her words. "I almost lost you and my father. What if something were to happen to one of us during the night? Then I'd never know how it feels to be well loved by you. Never know how it feels to make love with you." Annie swiped a tear from her eye. "If something happened and I lost you, I'd never marry, Cane. There's no one else I want."

Frowning, he sank back on his heels. She leaned toward him, hands stretched out. He grasped them and said, "Have you had another premonition? Didn't I tell you to let me know if you did so we can—"

"No. No premonitions, Cane. I just don't want to wait any longer."

"Damn, neither do I," he said, pulling her to her feet. He locked the door. Then, taking her in his arms, he kissed her, even as he undressed her hurriedly. She eagerly waited for him to take her again in his arms, but he didn't. He just looked at her standing before him, clad only in her bloomers, chemise and stockings. She saw the raw desire on his face as he gazed upon her. He reached out and untied the ribbons on her chemise.

Cane's flaring nostrils and the hot-eyed look made her shiver. He moved slowly, increasing her anticipation.

My God! Make love to me!

As if he could read her mind, he picked her up in his arms and laid her down on the divan. He positioned her with her head on one of the arms. He removed her chemise and her bloomers, and she blushed to the roots of her hair.

"Beautiful," he whispered with reverence.

He splayed her legs apart until the sole of one of her feet was on the floor while the other remained bent on the divan seat. Then, standing there, he simply looked at her in pure passion.

Suddenly, she had misgivings and opened her mouth to stop him, but Cane leaned down and took her lips. She felt him beside her then. He was on his knees, at her side.

"I never did thank you for accepting my proposal, Annie." He looked up and she saw the love in his eyes. "But I'm thanking you now. Unfortunately, I haven't had a chance to get you a ring yet, but..."

"It doesn't matter, Cane. It doesn't. Now make love to me."

Annie lay there on the divan like a wanton as she watched Cane undress. Her eyes settled on every part of him, unable to believe his masculine splendor, for he indeed was more beautiful than any man should ever be.

He settled down upon her. He kissed her in places she never dreamed possible, carrying and culminating her arousal to unbearable heights, and she burned for more.

Finally, she begged, "Now, Cane, please! End this torment."

Smoothly, he eased inside her. She felt only a momentary pain before she raised her legs and wound them around his waist, urging him deeper.

Cane gasped. "Oh, sweet Annie, you are something. It's been so long," he groaned. "I want this to be good for you, but I don't know if I can hold out for long."

"Take your pleasure, Cane," she whispered with a smile.

He did, but not before giving her pleasure. He made love to her, and she soared to the heavens and back with him. Afterwards, all she could think was how she'd die if she lost him. She wouldn't want to continue living without him. They dressed after making love.

Later, Cane wakened to the smell of fire. Then he remembered. They were in the library, door locked. The fire in the fireplace must still be burning low, he decided, closing his eyes again, reveling in the warmth of pretty Annie asleep in his arms.

The smell of fire grew stronger, more pungent, and Cane coughed. His eyes shot open then, closing just as quickly as he'd opened them. He rolled off the divan, eyes burning at the smoke filling the library. He coughed again and stumbled to the door. He touched the brass knob and yanked his hand away. "Shit!" It was hotter than a branding iron.

"Annie? Annie!" Cane shook her shoulder, but she hardly stirred. He checked the pulse in her neck.

Still breathing, thank God!

Shouting to alert the others in the house, he picked Annie up in his arms. He wrapped two woolen blankets around her but laid her back down on the divan again.

Grabbing a poker, he smashed a window until every jagged edge of glass was gone. Returning to Annie, he picked her up, climbed through the window, thankful they had been sleeping on the first floor. Just as he'd maneuvered them outside, something hit him on the head.

~ * ~

Annie gasped in the fresh air, her body shivering where she lay on the snow. She sat up, sobbing when she discovered Cane beside her. "Cane? Wake up, Cane!"

As she crouched over him trying to rouse him, she saw color in her side vision. Looking in that direction, she saw a man's boot just as it disappeared around the corner of the house.

Blood seeped from a cut on the top of Cane's head and one across his forehead. Looking skyward, she saw the house engulfed in flames. She picked up a large piece of wood and knew it was the piece that had felled Cane.

"Annie!"

"Father! Over here, outside the library window! Is Mark with you?"

Her father appeared from the back of the house, his face frantic. "No! I thought he was with you!"

"We've got to find him!" Clutching the blankets wrapped around her, she rose and started to run but her father hauled her back, keeping his grip on her.

"You can't go inside. The house is too far gone."

"But Mark! He has to be upstairs."

"I glanced in his room and most of the others before we left the house, and I didn't see him. I called to him, too, and there was no answer. I thought he was with you, or one of the hands took him out. Where else would he have gone?"

"I don't know, but we have to look for him."

"Not inside," her father said. "He's got to be outside somewhere."

Harvey, one of their hands, appeared. "Come into the barn," he shouted. Glancing at Cane, he said, "I'll get Paul to help me get him inside."

"We've another priority. Mark's missing. I want all hands out searching for him," her father said.

Annie stood in the cold, shivering, tears falling down her cheeks and freezing upon them.

Harvey said. "Come on, Miss Annie. We'll find the boy."

Two more hands arrived and carried Cane into the barn. Annie followed, searching for Mark along the way. The snow had stopped, but the temperature had fallen and the wind still blew. As she pulled the blankets tighter around her, she saw movement behind the barn.

As she rounded the barn, she saw a big man, head uncovered, blonde hair blowing as he mounted his horse.

"Hee-yah!" he shouted and spurred his horse into a gallop.

Chills tore through Annie as she put a name to the man, though she hadn't seen his face clearly. Jed Porter! Something lay in the snow, metal-colored, and she slowly approached it. She peered closely and saw a can of some sort, then reared back at the smell of kerosene. Dear God, Jed had set the fire.

Annie ran around to the front of the barn, looked up at the house, the porch below, and saw a figure at Mark's window. "Mark!" she yelled.

"Annie! Help me!" Mark mouthed.

Scampering as quickly as she could through the snow, her feet near frozen, she heard a roar. Looking up once more, she cried, "No!" as glass rained down from several windows in the house

Annie ran to the front door and opened it. She choked on the smoke that billowed outside. Pulling the wool blanket from her shoulders, she wrapped a tail of it around her head and another across her mouth, keeping her eyes uncovered. Racing around the back, she remembered the old sct of stairs, once used by servants in the household. The same stairs she'd scolded Mark for using. Praying the fire hadn't caught there yet, she rushed to the kitchen. She yanked at the old door's handle until it opened on the third try. Looking up the rickety old stairs, she was glad to see just a fine mist of smoke.

Annie called up the stairs, "Mark! Head to the old staircase, down by Pa's room."

She heard him sobbing out her name.

When he didn't appear, she shouted again, "Mark! I'm in the kitchen!" She kept calling him until she heard his footsteps overhead drawing near.

He appeared at the top of stairs, then clattered down them, coughing and sobbing at the same time. He flung himself into her arms. "I was afraid, Annie, so I hid in my closet."

"I know. I'm glad you followed my voice. Come on, we have to get out of here."

They reached the kitchen when an explosion rent the air. Annie screamed as chunks of the roof started falling down on them. Dense smoke poured into the kitchen. Pulling Mark with her, she ran to the kitchen door just as a flash of fire ignited the wallpaper, then flamed around the door, blocking their exit. She groaned, seeing the only escape route was the window high above the stove. Both of them were too short to reach the window, even standing on the stove, but she might be able to hoist Mark onto her shoulders and ease him through it. The danger of the fall he'd be taking to the ground outside made her look for other options.

In the living room, she saw nothing but flames. A hissing sound over her shoulder prompted her to look back in time to see the parlor curtains burn up faster than dried tinder. Then she remembered the kitchen pantry. It might offer them protection if they couldn't get outside—until someone found them. Or it would be their final resting place. If nothing else, at least she could give Mark some peace in his final minutes.

It was their only chance. Dragging Mark along, both of them coughing, they stumbled into the kitchen again. Annie pulled on the pantry door. The cedar-lined room was stacked with food supplies, free of smoke and fire for the moment. She cleared out a corner, closed the door tight and sank to the floor, pulling Mark down with her.

"Annie?"

She looked down, barely making out the glint of his eyes in the darkness.

"Are we gonna die?"

"No, we're not."

Please, God.

The stinging in her eyes subsided and the coughing as well. The pantry door seal at the floor was fairly tight and kept out most of the smoke.

"I'm tired," Mark complained.

"Then close your eyes and lean against me. We'll rest a bit."

As the boy fell asleep, and then her own eyes started closing, she prayed somehow someone would put out the fire, or come for them.

65

~ * ~

"Where are they?" Cane shouted.

"We've looked everywhere," Callahan said, sounding defeated.

No! I won't lose my family now that I've finally found them.

He'd been searching for Annie and Mark himself for what seemed like forever, with no success. He paused and stared at the burning house, knowing it was lost. Could Annie have gone back inside to search for Mark? He prayed she hadn't, but knowing Annie's love for the boy exceeded all things, including her safety, he realized he had only one choice but to go inside.

He ran toward the house, whipping around when Callahan called out to him. "Cane! She wouldn't have gone back inside!"

"I have to see for myself," Cane replied. His voice was cold and uncompromising. He wouldn't allow anyone to stop him.

Fire blocked his path through the front door. He ran around to the library window. More fire. He needed something to protect himself, so he returned to the barn. There was a horse trough filled with water that was frozen.

No good, damn!

He paused, feeling the other men's eyes on him, watching him in silence. Snow would work. He tore a blanket down from a peg and ran back outside. He covered it with the heavy snow, waited a minute, then rubbed the moisture into the wool, hoping it was wet enough to afford him the protection he required.

Whipping the wet blanket around him, he ran to the back side of the house, to the kitchen area. He stood there shivering. When he touched the kitchen doorknob, it was hot. Callahan appeared. "Step back, Callahan," he said.

He saw smoke and fire inside through the window, but he had to go in. Bracing himself, he flew against the door, dodging to the left and falling to the snow. The damage the fire had already caused weakened it, and it crashed in while a backdraft explosion of heat and flames rushed out.

Fire spread across the kitchen. He heard whimpering then coughing. Whirling around, he followed the intermittent sounds, shouting, "Mark!

Annie!"

No reply, but he heard more coughing and followed it until he stopped outside the pantry door. His hand burned when he touched the doorknob, and he pulled it back. "Shit!"

Grabbing a hank of the blanket, he covered his hand and grabbed the knob once more. He yanked it open and, as he stood in the doorway, his heart filled with joy. Mark and Annie sat slumped on the floor against a wall. Praying they were alive, he squatted and checked their breathing.

They were alive! He reached to take Mark, but Annie suddenly opened her eyes—eyes filled with horror.

"You can't have him! You can't!" she screamed, hugging Mark close.

She appeared to be awake, but Cane believed she was asleep or in the midst of another premonition.

No time to think or reason with her now!

He wrenched Mark from her arms.

She moaned, "No, no! You can't take him."

Not wasting any time with words, Cane backed out of the pantry with Mark. He saw Callahan standing just outside the kitchen door. "Mark, Grandpa's right outside. Go to him."

Mark was groggy and ignored Cane's command, shouting, "Annie! Annie, don't let him…"

Cane smacked Mark's cheek and shook him. "It's me, your Pa, and Grandpa's here, so go on!"

His shouts and slaps startled but alerted Mark to his surroundings. Confusion filled his face as he stared at Cane. "Pa?"

If a heart could break, it would be his. *Damn!* His words had slipped out accidentally, and now Mark needed to be told. He prayed Annie wouldn't be angry, but there was no turning back now.

Urgency prevailed once more. "Get outside now. Grandpa will help you. I'll help Annie."

"I don't have no grampa!" Mark wailed as he tore outside.

Cane returned to the pantry. Annie fought him, screaming in his ear, flailing her arms and wind-milling her legs. "Shh, it's me, darling," he whispered, trying to hold her against him. "Wake up, damn it."

She slumped in his arms and tears poured from her eyes as she stared at him unbelievingly.

67

With a sob, she latched onto him. "You were the man in my vision, Cane, only you were trying to *save* us. The evil I felt was the fire."

Hauling her into his arms, he strode out of the pantry.

"Later," he said brusquely. He rushed outside. Mark and Callahan stood with worried faces, watching for them to exit. The sizzling he'd heard earlier happened again, and Cane snatched Mark up in his arms and hauled Annie along with him.

"Run!" he called to Callahan.

Callahan came behind and helped Annie. Together, they ran across the yard to the barn, then stopped and saw the house walls crumble and the roof tumble inside, the timber creating more tinder for the fire.

Annie sobbed. "Our house! Oh, Father, what are we going to do? And our possessions—all gone."

Callahan swiped soot from his face. "But we have our lives, every one of us, and that's a blessing."

Annie shivered as tears streamed down her cheeks. Cane stood beside her, his arms around her. "Honey, we have to go into town. Hopefully, Katie can find room for us at her place."

Teeth chattering, Annie nodded. All of them loaded up into two wagons and headed for Bozeman. The road was packed with snow, rough and uneven, but thankfully, the storm had passed. By the time they arrived outside The Palace, they were all frozen. Cane was worried about Annie and Mark since neither of them had any feeling in their fingers and toes.

James rushed out of the saloon and, without a word, hustled them inside. James and Katie made room for all of them. Callahan's hands had their own rooms at The Palace, to which they retired in exhaustion.

When Mark was resting, Cane sat with Annie. "You can cry, honey," he said softly, kissing her thawing fingers.

She sniffed. "I don't want to scare Mark."

"Mark had all of us hovering over him to keep him warm as we could. He's fine."

Annie nodded and allowed a few tears to streak down her cheeks. She closed her eyes and leaned back against the divan in Katie's parlor. Exhaustion unlike any she'd ever felt overwhelmed her. She snuggled into his strong, safe arms, felt herself being lifted but was too tired to respond. Warm blankets covered her, and she fell asleep.

Cane carried her up to one of the Palace's bedrooms and he stood over her, watching her for a while, until he was sure she was sleeping soundly, then left for his own room.

~ * ~

She wakened in the dark of the night, crying out even as another vision came to her. She was staring out the library window in her home, watching in horror as Jed Porter poured liberal streams of kerosene over the ice and snow, then struck a match.

She screamed in time with the first explosion and sat up straight in her bed. Cane was there and pulled her into his arms from where he sat beside her.

James burst into the bedroom and stood in the doorway. "What happened?"

"Annie had a vision, that's all, or maybe a nightmare," Cane replied.

"No!" Annie looked between the two of them. "I have always had the visions *before* an event happened. This time, I experienced it afterwards. Jed Porter set the fire at our house, James. I saw him!"

Frowning, James moved closer to her. "You saw him where? When?"

"In the vision, yes, but I saw him when we were back there, after we got out of the burning house. I saw him escaping on his horse, but I couldn't dwell on it. I had to look for Mark," she said. "In my vision, just a second ago, he set the fire. N-No one actually saw him set the fire, though, so it'll be his word against mine, won't it?"

"Afraid so," James said, "but I believe you and your visions. You may think of it as a curse, but honey, it's a gift. It truly is. Of course, it would help if we can find some evidence or proof since folks don't want to believe in your "gift." Try and get some more sleep."

"I saw a kerosene can by the barn—it wasn't one of ours. Oh, what in the world is wrong with Jed? My God, we've been friends forever! How could he do something so awful? I can't believe how much hatred he has for me," she sobbed.

Cane knelt beside her. "He was in love with you, Annie, and sometimes love can make people do awful things, especially when they realize their love isn't reciprocated. Mostly, though, love is the most wonderful thing that can happen to a person. I know, because I've found

69

love with you, sweetheart."

He took her into his arms then and held her as she cried.

~ * ~

The following morning, Cane, James and his two deputies rode out to retrieve the gas can Annie mentioned, then went to question Jed. Ironically, he had no witnesses to vouch for his whereabouts last evening. Even his ranch hands confessed to not knowing. The gas can matched several others in his barn. James brought him in and locked him up, saying Jed could rot jail until the circuit judge came to town. Arson was a serious crime, and he intended on forcing a confession out of the man.

James conferred with Cane's testimony of having heard Jed's fury and complaints to others in town that Miss Annie hadn't accepted his marriage proposal, instead choosing to marry a criminal. Of course, he'd already had to put Jed in jail once because he couldn't accept that Annie didn't want him.

One of the deputies noticed snow prints in the fresh fallen snow, around the Callahan family's barn and house, prints that matched Jed's boot size perfectly, but then, many men in the area wore the same size boot as Jed. And then, positive evidence was found; a small, silver cigar case with Jed's name engraved on it. A confession wouldn't be needed after all.

That night, Cane, Mark and Annie sat at Katie's dining room table with her family and ate beef stew and cornbread, a moroseness filling the air.

Cane noticed Mark's typically upbeat disposition wasn't so happy. "What's the matter, son?" he asked.

"We don't have no house, no more, no clothes—nothing—but you know what's really bad? The best Christmas tree we ever had is gone."

Katie patted Mark's hand. "Christmas will still happen. Only you'll be celebrating with us, here, if that's all right with you."

Mark nodded and swiped self-consciously at a stray tear.

Callahan took Mark onto his lap as the boy sobbed harder. "James, Katie," Callahan said, "We can't thank you enough for taking us in. But it might be a while longer than you think since the soonest we can start building a house is spring.

Katie laughed. "I'd love the company. So would James. And we will enjoy the merriest of Christmases together."

"Mark," Callahan said, "we need to talk with you about something else."

Katie and James wisely left the dining room to allow them privacy.

Mark's eyes widened on Callahan. "He said you were my grampa! I told him I ain't got no grampa, just you. You're my pa!"

Cane saw the sorrow in Callahan's eyes and stepped in to help. "Mark? You know you were adopted when you were a baby."

"Yup. Pa said my ma died."

"She did. I loved your ma—a lot. I made my way from Texas to Bozeman every year, driving cattle, and met your ma here. When I left for Texas again, I had planned on it being the last time 'cause I asked your ma to marry me. She would have if she hadn't died right after you were born. Then I got into some trouble in Texas and couldn't return—until I came earlier this year. I didn't know anything about you being born for a long time. I had no idea I had a son, but as soon as I did learn, I came right here. I want you to live with me 'cause you're my son. We look a lot alike. You said so, remember?"

Mark started crying. Between the tears, his voice trembled. "But I don't wanna live with you! I wanna live with Pa and Annie."

Annie said, "Mark, you know me and Cane are getting married soon. Cane...your pa...asked Grampa to live with us. We'll build a big house, and we'll all be together. You'll have all of us, all of the time. How does that sound?"

Relief flooded Mark's face. "Real good," he said, wiping the tears on his cheeks with his shirtsleeve.

Cane smiled. "You don't have to call me Pa, at least not until you get used to me. I'm hoping you learn to like me soon, son."

"I do like you, Mr., uh...Pa."

Cane's heart lurched at the shy look on his son's face.

"I love you, Mark. I feel real bad I missed out on so much of your life. I plan on making up for all that lost time."

Annie took his hand and he turned to her. "And, God willing, I hope we have children, brothers and sisters for you, son."

"Holy cow! I always wanted a brother! No sisters, though," Mark

71

said, his eyes pleadingly looking at Annie then Cane.

"But you love Melanie, don't you? She's a girl," Annie said.

"Yeah, she's okay," the boy said grudgingly.

"Sorry, son, only God is in control of that, not us."

~ * ~

On December 20th, Cane and Annie were married in the First Lutheran Church in Bozeman. Katie gave her friend her own wedding gown to wear. To Cane's mind, as Annie walked down the aisle toward him, he believed she'd look every bit as beautiful wearing a potato sack.

A reception was held at Katie's Palace, and the wedding feast was sumptuous. Cane couldn't recall ever having eaten so much and so well.

By nine o'clock that evening, Cane was growing weary of the guests that still lingered.

At ten, James took Cane's silent hint and proceeded to escort folks out of Katie's Palace.

By eleven, Cane finally got to make love to his new bride.

~ * ~

Later that evening, Annie lay beside her husband. She sighed, thinking how wonderful love was. She wore only her white silk stockings and frilly garters. Cane had insisted she keep them on, saying how they fired his blood. She grinned into his chest as heat stole through her body. It had fired more than just his blood and hers.

She thought about how handsome he looked, whether in his jeans a simple shirts or in the black suit, brocaded vest, white shirt and string tie and Stetson he wore today for their wedding.

"You are a wonderful husband, Cane, and I can hardly wait for us to build our house together and raise our children there."

Cane's eyes filled with tears. "I love you, Annie Smith. Never forget it."

"I won't," she said and kissed him again, cementing their promises to each other.

"Do you foresee a happy future for us, Mrs. Annie Smith?" he asked with a smile.

She closed her eyes and concentrated, tormenting him just a little.

Slowly, she replied, "Yes, I envision the happiest future anyone could have."

"I've found heaven, a reason for living, with you, my son, and any other children God gives us. This Christmas of 1888, I'll remember with perfect clarity for the rest of my life."

"So will I, my love." Giving him an innocent little smile, she said, "I think I'm through talking. For now."

"What about screaming?" he growled softly. "Bet I can make you scream."

"You can't, you won't!" she said on a giggle.

Pressing against his chest, she tried levering herself up off him, but he wouldn't allow it. She relaxed after he gently kissed her neck. "Well, perhaps a little scream or two would be okay."

She heard him chuckle as he rolled them over until she was beneath him—exactly where she wanted to be.

THE END

COMING SOON!
Jane and the Judge, A Montana Women Novella
Excerpt:
Chapter One

December 1888
Butte, Montana

"Quiet!" Judge Simon Hopkins ordered, pounding his gavel on the hardwood table that served as the bench of law in Butte and Bozeman, Montana. Simon was the only circuit judge to appear in Bozeman one month, then in Butte, the next. Having given his one warning, loud voices dropped to murmurs.

He hated the atmosphere today—eagerness mixed with anticipation— for folks in Butte knew everyone appearing today had been arrested for prostitution.

"Baliff, first one?" Simon said, directing his gaze at his assistant, Jordan Peterson.

Mrs. Jane Miller, rise," Peterson announced.

When Simon had first read the sheriff's report of the crime, he'd found it difficult to believe a married woman would prostitute herself, but then he saw that her husband was deceased, which meant she'd likely been left destitute.

Simon shoved his spectacles higher on his nose and looked up to see a tall woman in her mid-twenties standing before him. Her black hair she'd pulled back severely from her face and she wore widow's weeds. Looking closer, Simon saw wisps of curls framing her face. The bit of fluff softened her features. Her lips were closed tight, her small chin pointy and slightly defiant.

Good. The woman was a fighter. She'd need to be.

"Mrs. Miller, have you legal representation?"

She gaped at him and he felt more than a bit foolish. He guessed she didn't have a lawyer because she couldn't afford one—yet it was a standard question he asked everyone before sentencing.

"Yes, she has, your honor," a loud voice from the back of the courtroom called.

Simon saw a stocky man, slightly receding hairline, forty or so. He was dressed well, in a fine brown summer weight suit and he used an ebony cane as ornamentation rather than need. He was also sweating profusely. Simon caught the heated look in the man's eyes as he looked at Mrs. Miller and knew the man possessed unsavory thoughts about her.

"No!" Mrs. Miller declared. "He's not my lawyer but my husband's brother who only wants—"

She didn't finish her response but looked away, that chin held high once more.

Simon met her hazel-colored eyes that begged him to understand why she didn't finish speaking. Beneath her deceivingly plain appearance was a beauty, one who'd fallen on hard times. "He wants what?"

After a long while, when she didn't reply, he prompted, "Mrs. Miller?"

"Me," she whispered, looking down at her hands which she kept twisting in front of her.

Simon nodded at his bailiff.

Peterson looked at the man standing in the back of the courtroom.

74

"Proceed to the bench, sir."

The man walked swiftly to the front, stopping beside Mrs. Miller, who seemingly cringed away from him.

"Your name?" Simon demanded.

"Clive Miller. Mrs. Miller was married to my brother, Robert."

"Has Mrs. Miller hired your services? Are you a solicitor?"

"I am an attorney, your honor, but alas, Mrs. Miller has too much pride to take up my offer. My poor sister-in-law has been distraught since my brother's demise, and not thinking clearly."

"That's not true," she said in a trembling voice.

"It seems the lady has a difference of opinion. She has obviously refused your offer, so that's that. You may sit down."

"But your honor—"

Simon's eyes riveted on the man. "You heard me, now sit down, or leave."

The man stalked out of the courtroom, murmurings following in his wake.

"Order!" Simon slammed his gavel down on the desk.

The voices subsided. Looking over the top of his spectacles, Simon asked, "Are you pleading not guilty, Mrs. Miller?" Poking his finger at the report in front of him, he added, "It seems there's more than one witness to your crime at the White Pearl Saloon. Do you deny that? If so, then we go to trial. If not, then I will proceed with sentencing."

"I am guilty," she whispered, "but not of the act itself."

"Finish, please," Simon demanded, though he kept his voice soft and gentle. He knew precisely what she meant, but he had to hear her say the words, though they wouldn't clear her. Even if she hadn't bedded a man she'd been caught with intent to do so.

"We hadn't fornicated yet."

About the Author

Nancy Schumacher is the owner-publisher of Melange Books, LLC, writing under the pseudonyms, Nancy Pirri and Natasha Perry. She is a member of Romance Writers of America, and one of the founders of the Minnesota RWA chapter, Northern Lights Writers (NLW).

www.nancypirri.com
https://www.facebook.com/NancyPirriAuthor

Other works by the Author

Night Magic in Romance and Mystery Under the Northern Lights Anthology
To Tame A Gambler in Western Ways Anthology
A Little Holiday Magic, author anthology
Make Me Behave (An Anthology) with Tara Fox Hall

Bait Shop Blue
The MacAulay Bride
Ruined Hearts, writing as Natasha Perry
All I Ever Wanted
I Wish You Love, a Spicy Romance Anthology
Annie and the Marshal, A Montana Women Novella

Coming Soon!
Jane and the Judge, A Montana Women Novella

www.ingramcontent.com/pod-product-compliance
Lightning Source LLC
Chambersburg PA
CBHW031900170626
46807CB00004B/1817